The Fifty-Fifty Feeling

Written by
Karin König

Translated by
Louisa Barnett, Kitty Geddes, and
Lizzie Scott

Bloomington, IN   Milton Keynes, UK

authorHOUSE®

AuthorHouse™
1663 Liberty Drive, Suite 200
Bloomington, IN 47403
www.authorhouse.com
Phone: 1-800-839-8640

AuthorHouse™ UK Ltd.
500 Avebury Boulevard
Central Milton Keynes, MK9 2BE
www.authorhouse.co.uk
Phone: 08001974150

First published by AuthorHouse 2/12/2007

ISBN: 1-4208-8277-5 (sc)

Printed in the United States of America
Bloomington, Indiana

This book is printed on acid-free paper.

From the Author

Approximately eighteen months ago I received a letter from Diana Hughes, German teacher at Tudor Hall. She not only wrote that her pupils had been reading my book 'Ich fühl mich so fifty-fifty' in their German lessons, but also that they were translating the story into English and had found a publishing company for it.

I was very happy to receive the invitation to come to London for the launch of the book. Our meeting took place at the Oxford Street branch of Waterstones. I saw the book cover gleaming out from the shelves, and I had not imagined that it would be done so professionally. In addition to the initiator, Diana , I met the translators, Kitty, Lizzie and Louisa, who had, in the meantime, left school and were, it seemed to me, at home all over the world.

The book not only has a very attractive appearance, but it has been translated most professionally. An American translator, a colleague at the Hamburg Institute of Social Research, confirmed my impression of how topical the translation is. A slight modernisation of the language - after all, I wrote the book sixteen years ago - has enhanced the text.

I would like to thank everyone involved for their work on the English version, and I hope that I will find many more readers in your country.

Karin König .
Hamburg, November 2006.

Chapter 1

"Why have I brought along cowards like you? Switch off the torch at once!" Furiously Sabine turns to Stefan and Jürgen. "We're on the run, and not on a scouts' expedition for little boys."

"Sorry, but we thought…" comes back the barely audible reply.

"I just don't understand it. They've caught you twice already. This time you're dragging me into it too."

There is no answer, but Sabine can really sense the fear of the two of them. One of them stumbles. There is a treacherous cracking sound, a slight groan. "Damn it, my foot."

"My goodness. We've only just started out! How should this…oh, sugar!" Sabine has run into some barbed wire. They climb carefully over it.

'At least we're going in the right direction', she thinks.

The path through the woods ends abruptly. The three of them grope their way forwards…Sabine switches on the torch, but holds her coat protectively over the beam. She gets the compass from her trouser pocket.

"North, we're going in the right direction."

"Do you really think so?" asks Jürgen anxiously.

"Yes, but you're welcome to go south."

"No," whispers Jürgen, "but we can't go any further this way."

Sabine has to admit he is right. The wood is getting more and more dense. Thorny bushes block their way. Nature has formed an impenetrable wall. The three of them stop, uncertain as to what to do. It starts to drizzle lightly. It is August but it feels cold.

"We must get through this wall of bushes somehow." Sabine tries to talk herself into being brave. Determined she presses on, feeling for gaps.

"We can only crawl through, force our way through. Luckily we haven't got any luggage with us."

Partly on all fours, partly slithering along on their stomachs, they fight their way through the undergrowth. Cynically, Sabine thinks that the military training that they had to do during their time at school is proving to be exceedingly useful. Scratched and exhausted, they eventually reach a path through the wood. Sabine switches on her torch briefly.

"Tyre tracks, my God, that's the border guards!"

"Perhaps that's the path we were on before," whispers Stefan.

"We're bound to have been going around in circles. Come on, let's go!" says Jürgen in a quavering voice.

"Whatever, I'm going to look for the second barbed wire fence." Sabine tries to make her voice sound firm. Dejectedly the three of them walk along the path through the wood.

"There's a light over there. That must be the border soldiers."

"But which ones? Austrian or Hungarian?"

"Perhaps they're refugees, like us?"

"We could give them a signal with the light," considers Jürgen.

"You've been watching too much West TV."

Sabine suddenly becomes alert. She is convinced that they are at the second border fence; it is just as it had been described to her. However, with one difference. It is as high as a house. Her eyes fill with tears. She feels totally alone. Exhausted she leans against the barbed wire. There is a cracking behind her, she feels the wire give way under the pressure of her body.

"Wow! The wire is fragile! We could bend it apart."

"Don't shout so much, do you want the border soldiers to come and help?" Jürgen interrupts Sabine.

They break a large hole in the wire without any trouble, and climb through.

"We wouldn't have such a dilapidated fence back home." There is something like pride in Jürgen's voice..

"What do you mean, 'back home'?" asks Sabine sharply.

All three laugh. 'Back home.' Where was that? Perhaps it would soon be the Bundesrepublik, provided that they weren't caught.

"But the Hungarians won't hand us back to the *DDR," thinks Sabine out loud, more to comfort herself.

---

* DDR Deutsche Demokratische Republik, the former East Germany.

Then it occurs to her that Jürgen and Stefan have already had this experience twice before.

"I'm not going to not let myself be caught again," says Jürgen with conviction.

"You can tell them that," replies Stefan mockingly.

"Perhaps they'll throw you straight into a loony bin, for so much stupidity." Sabine does not actually mean to be so angry, but she is too exhausted to be friendly. Stefan and Jürgen do not reply. They notice how shattered Sabine is. For a while all three are silent. In the meantime the drizzle has eased. Stars are shining in the sky. "There's no point in going on," says Sabine in despair, "Perhaps we're going around in circles. We must wait until it's light. Come on, over there is a raised hunters' hideout, we won't be found so quickly there." Sabine climbs the ladder to the raised hideout. Jürgen and Stefan follow her in silence. Once at the top she sits on the floor exhausted, a wooden wall provides something to lean against. Using the light from her torch she looks at her watch. 3 o'clock.

"We've already been on our way for four hours", says Stefan distributing biscuits. "They're from the Intershop."[1] All three laugh quietly about it. "Intershops," says Sabine dreamily. "There's one around the corner at home in Leipzig. There's such wonderful milk chocolate, filled with marzipan, not to mention Yoguretta. It makes my mouth water."

"At home in Schwerin, it's really pathetic, but the Intershops in Berlin are like nothing you have ever seen

---

[1] 'Intershops' were shops in which one could buy goods from the West using Western currency.

in your life. They have everything. Even the Bundis shop there and that's saying something." Stefan really gets going. "Just imagine Bine, they sell pocket calculators which are as small as a matchbox."

"Now you can get everything first-hand in the West," replies Sabine.

"Only I have no money, fifty East German marks which won't get me very far. Do you think one can get work over there? It's supposed to have become difficult with so many East German refugees." Stefan falls silent, depressed.

"You can go back and become a soldier on the border," replies Jürgen. "We left because we didn't want to join the army. But perhaps then you'll get enough money for a pocket calculator. Perhaps you'll get extra danger money at the border." Jürgen's voice almost cracks with emotion.

"You're right," admits Stefan "Calm down. I didn't mean it at all. I've never had Western money, I have no Western relatives, no connections, nothing."

Sabine is only half listening. She has had this conversation too many times before. Now that she is sitting calmly she feels her exhaustion. Her hands are scratched, her right ankle aches, she must have twisted it. The whole situation seems absurd to her. 'What am I even doing here?' She thinks. 'Why aren't I sitting comfortably at home in my bedroom in Leipzig, instead of crouching, freezing, on a hunter's lookout on the Austro-Hungarian border? How shall I explain to them over there why I fled to the West? Actually, what is 'over there'? East or West?' she broods. 'To be honest, I never wanted to leave. Especially now that everyone is going.'

Sabine is suddenly wide-awake. How she would have liked to see herself as a lone warrior, always courageous in representing her opinion at school. Admired by classmates, feared by the teachers. 'I've never behaved like that in any situation,' she admits to herself. She doesn't want to deceive herself, not any more. 'Despite this,' she thinks and clenches her fists in her trouser pockets. 'Despite this, I would have stayed in the DDR,' Her eyes flood with tears. 'If the business with Mario and Mutti hadn't happened.'

Her thoughts wander back. She is in Leipzig again. The calendar goes back six months. Sabine remembers.

Chapter 2

"Don't forget to pack the illustrated book about Leipzig. Tante Gerda will be pleased about that. Perhaps she'll feel like visiting us then."

Laughing, Sabine throws the brightly gift-wrapped book to her brother. Sabine's mother joins them. Tenderly she strokes her son's hair. "Are you looking forward to the trip?" Mario finds his mother's caress unpleasant in the presence of his mocking, grinning sister.

"Of course," he mumbles, "of course I'm looking forward to Hamburg, but not to Tante Gerda." He imitates her hurt-sounding voice, "Well you know, Mario, I don't go to East Germany, so you must come to me."

She speaks like this on the telephone every time. Tante Gerda is the wife of Uncle Franz, Sabine's father's brother. Uncle Franz died a few years ago. As Mario is Tante Gerda's godson, she has invited him to her 60th birthday in Hamburg. For Mario, this birthday is the first opportunity to apply for a visitor's visa to the Federal Republic. Nobody thought that Mario would get a travel permit. However, it worked. He is allowed, for a week, to leave the DDR to go to Hamburg. Sabine looks at her brother a little enviously. Although she doesn't begrudge him his trip, how she would have liked to go with him. "Just to travel once to the West," she sighs. "Just to have a look, that's all. Why isn't that possible?"

"Ask your Stabu* teacher that tomorrow. She's sure to know the right answer," retorts Mario and shuts his case with a flourish.

"I'm not ready to die! As if you had ever asked a question like that in school," Sabine is cross. Mario always makes out that she's a coward. He can talk; after all he's finished with school. She still has to pass her Abitur. Oh well, these few months will also pass. She will not behave carelessly so close to her goal. Her father interrupts these thoughts by saying, "Come on, we must go, the train won't wait."

Arriving at the station, they look for the ticket counter 'Abroad.' "My dear brother is going abroad, to West Germany," jokes Sabine, and pinches her brother's arm. Mario grins at her.

At the 'Abroad' counter, business is brisk.

"A ticket to Hamburg," demands Mario, when it is finally his turn.

"What?" comes the astonished reply. Somewhat edgily Mario repeats his request.

---

* Staatsbürgerkunde was a subject taken from the seventh class onwards, in which political procedures such as Marxism were taught with great bias.

"Well, I'd like to see your passport," replies the ticket-saleswoman. "Or are you collecting the ticket for your grandmother? Then I can tell you right away, without a passport you don't get anything here."

Without replying Mario shows his passport. He had to apply for it just for the journey to Hamburg. In the meantime he had to hand in his ID card. After the trip he will get his ID card back, but at the same time the passport has to be returned. The people waiting around him look on curiously. Silently the passport is checked, silently Mario receives the ticket. During the payment not one unnecessary word is spoken. "She's never heard of the word 'friendliness'," says Mario, as they leave the ticket counter.

"Don't be annoyed. She's had her instructions," Sabine tries to calm him down. "Come on, we've got to go to platform 7. Our parents are waiting there."

"Why can't you buy a ticket to Hamburg without a passport here?"

"Don't make a mountain out of a molehill, especially not in front of our parents. Be happy that you're allowed to go. After all, you're the first in the Dehnert family."

"Allowed to, allowed to, that's all I hear. Well, if Mutti takes early retirement, she'll be able to as well," Mario's voice sounds a little more relaxed.

Platform 7 is very full. It is noticeable that almost only older people are getting on to the train. This is not surprising because DDR citizens who are not yet pensioners only get travel permits into the Federal Republic in exceptional circumstances.

"The Mummy Express," laughs Sabine's father. "It's really true."

In the meantime Mario has got on to the train and is waving from his compartment window. "Well guys, have fun," and turning to Sabine, "I'm sorry that I always tease you a bit but now you're rid of me."

"Well I won't exactly be getting withdrawal symptoms in one week," answers Sabine, laughing.

"Mario, seven days and not a minute longer!" Shocked, his mother puts her hand in front of her mouth.

"Nobody heard you." Sabine puts her arm round her comfortingly.

"Seven days, seven years, what's the difference?" Mario sounds a bit pretentious saying this. The train starts to move.

"Well, see you soon, somewhere." Mario waves and blows them a kiss.

"What a show-off." Sabine turns and secretly wipes the tears from her eyes.

Chapter 3

The telephone rings. Sabine lifts the receiver.

"Has Mario written?" she hears her mother ask breathlessly.

"No, I would have rung you at work if he had. Just don't get upset. Mario won't have been kidnapped. Perhaps he just wants to have a look at the West in peace, without Tante Gerda." Sabine tries to make her voice sound confident.

"But Tante Gerda said that she had put Mario on the train to Leipzig after a week."

"Mutti, she brought him to the station, not to the train. Tante Gerda had to go to the doctor. Mario probably didn't even get on the train to Leipzig." Sabine is getting impatient. How often have she and her father tried to calm her mother.

"But he didn't have any money." Her mother's voice breaks.

"But Mutti, he'll have got the 'welcome money' and Tante Gerda will have given him something too."

"You know Sabine, sometimes I think that Tante Gerda isn't telling us the truth. She knows where Mario is, and she isn't telling us."

"But why?"

"Because she doesn't want any trouble, or…"

"Or," Sabine interrupts her, annoyed, "because Mario doesn't want her to."

"Yes perhaps you're right." Her mother's voice is barely audible. There is a click on the line. Frau Dehnert has hung up.

"You beast, if you were standing in front of me I'd shoot you, my dear brother. You can be sure of that!" Sabine yells into the dead telephone line. "You don't need your Cabinet cigarettes any more, you can pump your lungs full of fine West cigarettes."

Furious, she throws the opened packet of cigarettes, which had been lying on the chest of drawers, into the wastepaper basket. Sabine feels the tears coming, not of fury, but of grief and desperation.

Her brother's departure has changed her life radically. That the departure is final is clear to everyone, including her mother.

"How could he explain showing up at the border and wanting to come back after four weeks? Mario knows that very well. But what if something has happened to him after all? An accident? Perhaps he's been attacked, got into bad company, is under the influence of drugs? Hamburg is such a big city, one could easily go under there. You can't rely on Tante Gerda, she only thinks about herself."

It started when Mario rang just once from Hamburg. OK, he doesn't like being mothered, but this was such an unusual journey. It was strange too that Tante Gerda had suddenly invited him. She had seldom been in touch since the death of her husband.

The obligatory Christmas parcel for the 'poor people in the Zone', impersonally packed by a supermarket, was about the only thing that reminded them of her. It was true, Mario was her godson, but he hadn't noticed that much. And then came this invitation out of the blue. Had Mario himself set this in motion? Perhaps he had asked Tante Gerda to invite him, and stressed that he wouldn't cost her anything. Had he already been planning to stay in the West?

Sabine is startled out of these thoughts. The doorbell rings, and at the same time the door opens. Herr Dehnert has come home.

"Well, heard anything from Mario?" he asks, and seems very tired. "No," Sabine strokes her father's arm comfortingly. Overnight he has become old, or so it seems to Sabine. Or hadn't she noticed before? Yesterday she wanted to fetch her father from the bookshop where he works. She wanted to cheer him up. But she got there too late, again. From a distance she could just recognize her father. Slowly and stooped, he was going along Katharinenstrasse. His head was hunched between his shoulders, his glance fixed on the ground. As if he didn't want to be seen or spoken to by anyone. The news that Mario had not returned from a visit to the West had spread like wildfire. "He's gone over," was the unanimous opinion.

Sabine is roused from her thoughts when she hears her father clattering about in the kitchen with the dishes.

"You've become a real house husband, come on, I'll dry up." Sabine takes a kitchen towel. "You know, Vati, that's a compliment."

"Well, now that Mario's not here anymore," mutters her father.

"Well he didn't exactly overwork himself as far as housework was concerned." Sabine dries up the cutlery.

"How are things going in school?"

"Oh, it's OK," Sabine replies slowly, and polishes the knives like a world champion.

"Do your teachers already know about it?"

"Mmm, definitely."

"And how did they react?" Herr Dehnert doesn't look up. For him the washing-up also seems absorbing.

"You can imagine. Frau Müller asked me sarcastically, if the rest of the family had already applied for an exit permit. She wants to speak to you both."

"That's what I thought." Herr Dehnert laughs bitterly.

"I hope they let me do the Abi. When the father of a girl in my class, Ulrike, stayed in the West, the teachers bullied her. In the end she and her mother had had enough and they applied for an exit permit too."

"Calm down, child. I'll explain to the school directors that it was Mario's decision to stay in the West. We didn't know anything about it." The door of the flat opens.

"Mutti's here," they both say at the same time, almost relieved. Frau Dehnert comes into the kitchen; she too seems tired and stressed. She puts her shopping bag on the chair.

"Sometimes I have the feeling that I spend my life standing in queues at the shops."

Sabine's mother loathes the daily shopping battle, especially when she comes home and sees the disappointed faces, when there hasn't been any decent fruit or vegetables to buy again.

"Well, anything new?" Frau Dehnert tries to make her face look as indifferent as possible.

"No," answers her husband quietly.

"What's for supper?" calls Sabine, as if she hadn't heard the question.

Chapter 4

"Mutti, don't you want any more to eat?"

"No, you eat," answers Frau Dehnert deep in thought. "It can't go on like this, this waiting is driving me mad. I really don't know how you can eat your supper so calmly. I find this uncertainty unbearable. Mario has never done anything like this before." Frau Dehnert gesticulates so violently that she almost knocks over her glass. "He's often disappeared suddenly, that time to Prague or last summer to Bulgaria. But he got in touch with us as soon as he could."

Sabine and her father exchange glances.

"I don't understand it. How often have we discussed in the past weeks whether we should put in exit requests. But we always come to the same conclusion: that we should stay. Mario thought the same, although he complained the most about the DDR."

"Christa, don't torment yourself so much." Worried, Herr Dehnert looks at his wife.

"Oh leave me alone. You always think I want to leave. It's true, too. How I'd love to travel to the South, where it's warm, where the oleander blossoms and the oranges grow. I'd like to see the Mediterranean, just once, Italy, Spain, Greece."

"Me too," Sabine agrees.

"Afterwards I'd come back straight away. Why doesn't my country trust me with this decision? We're treated like immature children. Come on, say something."

Searching for help, Frau Dehnert looks at her husband.

"Christa, you know very well that I was against going. Unlike you, I think we have a good life here. We have everything we need, a reasonable job, a lovely flat, our future is secure. Sabine, haven't you got a pretty room, plenty of friends? You can study soon. What else do you need?"

"Oh Vati, how can I explain it to you? You think Mario and I are ungrateful. It's not about that at all. We just miss being able to breathe freely. If you ask me, Mario always wanted to go, he just didn't dare to say so."

At this last sentence Herr Dehnert gives a start. Without a word, he gets up, stands there hesitantly and then says, almost embarrassed, to Sabine, "You know, perhaps I've never said it, but I'm very proud that you're going to be studying soon. I really wanted that for Mario," he says and then turns to the door. "Well, I'll go for a little stroll. I'll be back soon."

"Typical Vati, as if this little sermon is going to help us!"

Frau Dehnert shakes her head. "Sabine, I think it's high time that we had a talk about something."

"I couldn't bear another sermon this early in the evening," says Sabine sharply, but her mother appears not to hear.

"We've never told you about certain things, because we thought they would put too much of a strain on you. But I think that time is over." Frau Dehnert takes a deep breath.

"Sabine, I'm sure you are a bit puzzled by your father sometimes. His behaviour is often strange, I notice that quite clearly. When you were seven years old, Vati was at the peak of his career as a mineralogist. He was about to have his own institute, with twenty employees; he was going to put together a little museum, go on research trips to the West. The only condition was that he should join the Party. Vati refused, and suddenly there was no more talk of his being the director of the institute. What was worse for him though, was that he just didn't seem to exist any more for his colleagues. He didn't get any more information, he wasn't allowed to go abroad to do research, the museum wasn't opened. Later he found the job in the bookshop, and the rest you know. Since then Vati has changed. He's so quiet and reserved. Before, he used to be so full of life and sociable. At parties he was the immediate centre of attention. He loved his profession. He was proud of his country. But he didn't want to join the Party."

"But Mutti, the business with the Party has happened to so many people," says Sabine, "He should have known that."

"Well, yes," answers Frau Dehnert, "I think that since then Vati doesn't want any more problems with the DDR. He's found his own private niche, nothing's going to move him out of it any more. But he wants you two to have your own experiences with our country. He doesn't want to influence you. That's why we kept quiet, although it was often very difficult for me. Perhaps you understand your father better now?"

Frau Dehnert looks at her daughter hopefully.

"Yes, certain things are clear to me now and now I know too, why Vati gets so excited when he shows us his collection of stones. You can hardly stop him, he talks like a book and he's a completely different person." Sabine looks at her mother thoughtfully. "All the same, I think you should have told us the story before. Perhaps then Mario's relationship with Vati would have been better."

"You may be right," says Frau Dehnert quietly. "I'm so worried about Mario."

"Mutti, just getting upset isn't helping. If it's so important to you, you must try to go to Hamburg."

"I know, that's why I've tried to speed up my application for early retirement. Then I can go to the West legally, to Mario. I'm not going to let our family be destroyed by the border!" Frau Dehnert is visibly upset. "But now I need fresh air! Will you come with me, perhaps we can catch up with Vati?"

Chapter 5

Karin yawns, bored. "Where's Ramona, is she ill?" she asks her friend Sabine, whom she sits next to in class.

"No idea. Perhaps she doesn't want to come. But that's strange actually, so close to the Abi. Oh well, she can afford it, she's the best in the class after all."

Frau Müller, the class teacher, enters the room. The pupils stand up at once.

"Friendship." Her voice is neither friendly nor unfriendly.

"Friendship," answers the class in a monotonous voice.

"You can set the clock by her," whispers Sabine to Karin.

"It's true. Today she looks really smart, don't tell me she hasn't got contacts with the West. I'd like that purple spotted sweatshirt, you can't get that kind of thing here."

Frau Müller is considered by the class to be one hundred per cent, or as a through and through 'red'.

"Ramona Reuter will as from today no longer attend our school. Open your exercise books." Frau Müller's voice sounds even more impersonal than usual. She doesn't have to fear any questions about the whereabouts of Ramona. The pupils are much too afraid to attract attention so close to the end of school.

A numbed silence spreads through the class.

'Ramona has gone to the West and nobody had the slightest idea', thinks Sabine, and she is sure that her fellow pupils are thinking the same. 'I wonder whether her family applied for an exit request or if they got over the border illegally? Perhaps Ramona got away on her own?' Sabine looks across to Karin, their glances meet. 'Karin is bound to be thinking the same as me. Not that Ramona was our dearest friend, on the contrary. We always suspected her of being an absolutely committed Communist. Her mother was even a high-up party official and her father a 'Reisekader.'*

"I hope all went well for Ramona," Karin whispers to Sabine. "Are we the stupid ones, who stay behind?"

Sabine tries to get Karin to be quiet; Frau Müller must not hear such things!

"Only the stupid ones stay behind." This sentence resounds in Sabine's ears again and again. - 'No, we can't all go - I don't know anyone over there. Well, apart from Mario and Tante Gerda.'

---

* Kader were people who were responsible for leading the collectives in the socialist society. 'Reisekader' were allowed to travel to Western countries for certain reasons, such as academic meetings.

The lesson drags on, the thoughts of most of the pupils are with Ramona. She is the first in the class who has gone, but she is not the only one they know. Relatives, friends, neighbours, the baker round the corner, the children's doctor, one's best friend, are suddenly no longer there. Usually you get a brightly coloured postcard from them after a few weeks. Either from a West German city, from the Alps or from the North Sea, sometimes from Paris. The text on the cards is always the same. They write that they are having a wonderful time, that they already have a flat, a car and a job, and the first holiday abroad has already been booked. Then the contact dies down, on both sides.

'Well that's how it was with my cousin from Schwerin and with my mother's best friend,' Sabine thinks. 'Do they just forget us once they are over there? That seems to be the case with Mario.' The bell ringing for break startles Sabine out of her thoughts.

In the break they talk of nothing but Ramona's departure.

'It's always the same,' thinks Sabine. 'The ones who keep silent in class are the ones with the big mouths here.'

Fragments of sentences reach her ears. "We ought to show them - We ought to discuss it. – Anyway I'm not going to the army, I'd rather get out. Yesterday they showed on West TV that thousands of people had put in requests for exit permits, and nothing happened to them. Do you really believe that? My aunt lost her job the moment she applied to leave. -That's right, our neighbours too. Now they've been sitting on their packed suitcases for weeks and are waiting for their exit permits."

"Sabine, don't forget this afternoon," Karin reminds her.

"What are you two up to that's so important? Want to let me in on it?" Klaus, also known as 'the spy,' sidles up to them.

"It's only for girls, so unfortunately you can't be there," Sabine retorts

"Since when are only girls allowed to take part in church meetings?" Klaus grins shamelessly.

"Who said anything about church? Mind your own business." Karin pulls Sabine away. "Let's go in. Maths is starting".

At last school is over. The two friends have the same route home.

"You know," Sabine puts her arm through Karin's, "We're too cowardly to say to Klaus that we're going to the 'Junge Gemeinde,' because at least there we can say what we think."

"What's your problem?" Karin waves this aside, annoyed. "After all, you were the one who didn't want people to speak about it. You always told them we were going to town, or to the cinema, or some such rubbish. Apart from that, I don't want Frau Müller to find out what we do. Do you remember what she said about the pupils who took part in church activities?"

Sabine laughs and imitates her teacher's strict tones.

"A member of the church would also know how many wars were caused by the church."

"You see, she made them look really stupid, like warmongers."

"The worst part though, is that none of us defended them because we're always scared that we'll jeopardize our chances of a place at university or God knows what. Something really special ought to happen to shake us all up." Sabine is getting worked up, although she knows that Karin won't listen to her, and she doesn't even blame her.

Karin's eldest brother tried to leave the DDR illegally a year ago. He was caught in the act by border soldiers. When he resisted his arrest he was badly injured. The family was never given the details of the matter. This 'black sheep', as supposedly well-meaning class comrades called Karin's brother, caused the break-up of the whole family. The father, a staunch Communist, could not come to terms with his son's actions, and he later got divorced and moved to another town. Karin's mother changed her job, her elder sister turned down her university place out of protest at her brother's long prison sentence. She now works in an old people's home run by the church.

"Karin, how's your brother getting on?" Sabine turns to her friend.

"Mutti is allowed to visit him on Sunday. She's already quite sick with excitement. Have I told you that my father has got married again? A colleague, he told me. I wasn't to be angry if he chose to celebrate only with the closest family members. Well, I ask myself, who is that, if not me? Now I dream of the day when I tell his wife that her husband's son is in prison for attempting to flee the Republic. Perhaps she'll leave him post haste. It would be wonderful. I haven't told my mother about the wedding. I don't know if she could bear it." Karin stops. "Sabine, can you imagine that? A man turns his back on his family, just because his son wants to leave the country? Because he doesn't want to be a soldier or to study medicine, he wants to become a musician, best of all a drummer." Karin gesticulates wildly with her arms, imitating a drummer. She looks so funny that Sabine has to laugh out loud. Confused, Karin pauses. "What's funny about that?"

"Well, the way you were moving your arms."

"Don't you have anything else to say?"

"But Karin, I know the story by heart."

"So what? I haven't told you about the wedding before. It's like you with your Mario. I know that story backwards. Just wait and see how your family ends up. I'll be interested to see who'll disappear next!" Karin's voice breaks with anger. Unsure of herself Sabine looks at her. How should she answer? How dare Karin say that another member of her family is going to leave?

"Well, what if they do? At least my brother didn't behave as stupidly as yours."

Both girls look at each other speechlessly. They've never spoken like that to one another before.

'Damn', thinks Sabine. 'How could I say such a thing? I didn't want to hurt Karin. I'd better apologise.' Karin must be thinking the same thing, when she, fairly abruptly, murmurs, "I didn't mean it."

"Me neither," answers Sabine quickly.

They walk home together in silence. Suddenly Sabine notices that Karin is crying. For as long as they have known each other, she has never seen her friend crying. Hesitantly Sabine grasps Karin's hand and presses it gently. It feels cold.

"Karin, we're such stupid cows. You're my best friend and now you're walking beside me in tears." Impetuously Sabine hugs her friend. Karin cries even harder, and through her tears says, "I just can't take any more. I want to be happy too. At home there's always a miserable atmosphere My mother goes around with an embittered face, my sister talks of nothing but the old people's home, and my brother doesn't want to see any of us any more. Oh Sabine, you know, I'm seventeen, I want to go out dancing too, fall in love. But I'd feel so guilty, because of my mother."

Karin extracts herself from Sabine's embrace.

"It's not going to go on like this. After the Abi I'm getting out."

"Are you crazy? Where to?"

"Where do you think? Now that it's so easy to get to the West. You see, I'll do it! Well, see you this afternoon." Already Karin is round the corner. Speechlessly Sabine stops in her tracks. Since when has Karin wanted to go to the West?

Chapter 6

The church meeting room is almost too small for the environment group, which meets there once a week. The walls are painted in bright colours, slogans like 'Tschernobyl is everywhere' and 'Make peace, without weapons' can be read.

The room is sparsely furnished; damaged areas on the walls are covered with posters, which Pastor Adolph has brought back from a trip to the West. They are all posters about the destruction of the environment. "I smuggled them in under my robe," he laughingly tells the group.

The sticker 'We are staying here' is quite new and a product of the DDR. It has been given a prominent position, right under the wall clock.

Sabine arrives late again. The discussion is in full swing.

"Sorry to be late, but I've brought something with me."

She gets a packet of biscuits and a bar of chocolate out of her bag.

"Oh the good chocolate from the West! Your brother has been in touch. Sabine, are you lost to us? Chocolate, from an enemy of the state!" one of the group members comments in a good-natured way. They all laugh, Sabine too. Bernd, who is the leader of the group, continues, "Well, are you all agreed? We'll do a demo in front of the town hall to protest against the bad air in Leipzig. We'll tie cloths round our mouths. We must think up some stirring slogans for the posters. Yes, Renate, what do you think?"

"We can lie down on the pavement, as if we were dead, after an atomic accident. That's what they did in the West, after Tschernobyl. I saw it on West TV."

Sabine listens to them tensely. 'A demonstration, unbelievable. Such things are forbidden, and so they're dangerous. How come everybody's talking as if they're the most normal things in the world?' Sabine looks around at everyone. 'They all look very serious, but nobody looks afraid. Am I the only one who would rather shy away from this? Damn, such a short while before the Abi. There's something new every day. I should have stayed at home. Who's that new one over there? It's no coincidence that he's here, today of all days.'

"Has the new one introduced himself?" Sabine whispers to Karin, who is just putting a piece of chocolate into her mouth, with obvious enjoyment.

"That's Thomas. Doesn't he look sweet!"

"Well, he's OK. Such a torn jacket. His hair's like a field of stubble and then he's got metal-rimmed glasses too, just like the young Brecht in our schoolbook."

"Sabine, you are so bourgeois. You fit perfectly into our state. I like him." Karin grins in his direction. Thomas has noticed that he is being talked about. He winks at the two of them. Sabine looks away, furious. She doesn't like new people in the group. Who knows who might have sent him? The feeling of security, which she usually has in the group, disappears.

"Sabine, now calm down. Bernd brought Thomas with him. So he must be OK."

"We should all be aware that for us a demonstration like this wouldn't be without danger. We must reckon with having our IDs checked and registered. We mustn't go into this naively."

Sabine is annoyed; does it have to be the new one who expresses these doubts? The others agree that he is right.

"You're right Thomas, that's why we all have to be well prepared, Nobody outside the group must find out anything about our action."

Sabine knows that the air in Leipzig is polluted. She knows too, however, that this fact is officially denied. In school they had tried to bring up the subject once. The teacher had reacted skilfully, by demanding that they said where they had got the information. With that the subject was over. Even Frau Müller had shut the classroom window with the comment, "It stinks".

"When is it going to take place?" Sabine tries to make her question sound as casual as possible.

"Well," Bernd looks indecisively round. "We haven't talked about that yet. I think we need more specific information about the causes of air pollution.

I'll approach the people in Berlin, they've got experience with demonstrations."

It seems to Sabine as though the whole group breathes a sigh of relief. The delay seems to be welcomed by all of them. Many are about to do their Abitur. A demonstration like that could mean exclusion from the school. In any case there would be questions. The parents would be informed. Taking part in a demonstration is noted down in the Kaderakte* and accompanies one for one's whole life.

After the group meeting Sabine is sitting around with her friends. Everyone's relief that the action is not going to happen immediately, is noticeable

"Who feels like coming back home with me?" calls Renate. "I'm cooking spaghetti."

"Come on, let's go with them." Sabine pulls her friend's sleeve.

"Only if there's tomato sauce with it," answers Karin, laughing.

It is always like this. The friends visit each other constantly. Someone comes round, they eat together, listen to music, go to the cinema together, or to other friends. Renate's cousin Tanja visited her from the

---

* This personal file accompanied each DDR citizen from primary school onwards. One was not allowed to read it. The file remained with the Kaderleitung (in every company, in every institution in which people worked, there was a Kaderabteilung which is equivalent to today's personnel department). This was passed on internally from the school to training college, university or the company where one did one's apprenticeship and later to the work place.

West once, Sabine remembers, and she had found that somehow strange.

"You're always visiting each other, like with our Turkish neighbours." she said.

"Like with who?" None of them could begin to understand the comparison.

"When I visit my friend," explained Tanja," I call her first and ask if that's OK with her. Then we arrange a date. She has piano and ballet lessons, I go to jazz gymnastics and have to do a computer course. I do coaching, too, so I don't have much free time. If I went round to my friend's house without letting her know beforehand, and she wasn't there, I'd be very annoyed."

Sabine recalls how they had all looked at each other, perplexed. It was the greatest thing, to be together with your friends. Just like that. However, Tanja is right. As hardly any of them have got a telephone, they can't arrange meetings by phone. Sabine remembers exactly how delighted they had been at home, when they finally got their telephone. They had waited for it for six years.

Hardly any of the friends went to any courses. On the contrary, with all the compulsory school activities, frequently in the holidays too, they were happy when they could be together with their friends without any organising or planning. Strange, these Bundis, could one live there?

In any case, it had been very difficult to talk to Tanja. Somehow she had no problems in life. She always thought everything was OK, only she thought the DDR was incredibly boring. She thought the cars were pathetic, the department stores shabby, the cafes tasteless. She complained about the old-fashioned clothes the young people wore when they went to the Saturday disco. Renate had groaned, because she didn't know what more she could offer Tanja. Luckily they got West TV in Leipzig, but then Tanja had only complained about the few programmes they could receive. Strangely enough the only thing that she had been really crazy about was the trip to see Renate's grandparents in the region called the Altmark. She had been really enthusiastic about the cobbled, tree-lined country lanes, and the granny's little ponds. Yes, she thought everything was "just super". The group of friends didn't know what to think of her and were relieved when she finally set off for Hamburg.

'But why were we really all pleased, when Tanja finally left?' Sabine often thought about it. The friends had all felt so small and stupid next to her. Tanja had been everywhere already: Spain, to various Greek islands, and- unimaginably and unreachable for Sabine - her class was going to Paris in the autumn.

She hadn't dared to ask Tanja for postcards from Greece. Her friends would only have teased her about being bitten by the West bug. In the face of the Bundis one defended the DDR. It was quite strange, how they had all defended the DDR to Tanja, quite without having arranged to do so. They had all enthused about the fair school system, the cheap rents, bread being almost free. There was no unemployment, no drugs, no crime.

Her group, who were generally so hypercritical, were unrecognisable. Frau Müller would have been pleased. No wonder that Tanja defended the West.

There were no disagreements over music, they all knew the same things about that. However, there was a difference there. Contrary to them, Tanja had already seen a lot of groups 'live'. Hardly any West rock groups were allowed to come to the DDR. Only sloppy music for older people was allowed from the West. However, the DDR bands were great too, and naturally they were allowed into the West. Sabine had been in Berlin once, by the Wall. She wanted to hear a group that was playing on the West side. The music could be heard very well on the East side. But it was not to be. The police didn't even let the young people get near the Wall. The entire area was cordoned off. "We were chased away, without a reason. Can you imagine that?" she had asked her parents at the time, disgusted.

Chapter 7

Comfortably Sabine stretches under her blanket. Wonderful, it is already eleven o'clock. Stabu has already begun and she is lying lazily in bed. For no reason. Officially she is ill. Flu. Given the fine spring weather it is actually unusual, but this was simply Sabine's turn to be ill. Renate, Karin and Sabine had decided a year ago to skive once a month, taking turns, of course Today it was her turn.

Her mother looked quite worried this morning, when Sabine said to her that she was ill.

Sabine climbs out of bed.

"Let's see what the kitchen has to offer. What's going on here? The breakfast table is completely laid. The coffee's being kept warm, there are even two bread rolls." Touched, Sabine sits down at the coffee table. There is a little card propped up by the cup "Enjoy the food, enjoy the day, Mutti and Vati."

"Gosh, I have sweet parents, I just want to hug them." With a huge appetite she bites into a honey roll. After breakfast she has a long bath and washes her hair and tries to style her chestnut brown hair with gel borrowed from Karin, then she paints her nails bright red.

"Now to put the television on. Let's see what morning programme is on offer. I've really earned this free day, after the horror." Yesterday the time had come for her parents to see Frau Müller. Sabine already knew by heart the spiel she had come out with. Now that their son had left the DDR illegally, it had become clear that the correct political attitude was lacking in the parental home. They no longer came to the meetings of the Elternaktiv*. They should at least take care of their daughter, so that she wouldn't go the same way as their son.

The bell rings. Sabine pretends not to hear. The bell rings again, this time louder. Cautiously she peers onto the street. The delivery van. Sabine runs to the door of the flat, rushes to the door of their building and catches the postman just in time.

"About time. No school today and all dressed up? Here, this is for you, a parcel from the West. Is it unexpected?"

Sabine has known the postman for a long time, he is actually very nice, but unfortunately his son is in her class. She mutters, "I was just about to go to the doctor," and rushes away with the parcel. She has an idea who it could be from. Right, it is Mario's handwriting. Her heart beats loudly. She has to sit down, she is so excited.

---

* Elternaktiv: elected parental representatives of the school class.

"We must open the parcel together, but I could call Mutti quickly. Damn it, what was her office number?"

Whilst dialling Sabine's fingers tremble.

"Hello, yes I would like to speak to Frau Dehnert. What? Why isn't she there? Yes, I am her daughter. She should phone home at once What, she isn't coming back to the office? Thank you. Goodbye."

What does this mean, has Mutti also skipped work? She doesn't like calling Vati. He hates private conversations at work.

"My parents are definitely not going to return before seven. Whatever shall I do in the meantime?" Sabine turns off the television and tunes in the radio. She turns up the music full blast and waits for Frau Reuter to knock, which she promptly does. She is the only one in the house who does not work. Allegedly she doesn't need to.

Somehow the time passes. Sabine has tidied up, cleaned and prepared dinner. Around seven o'clock she turns on West television.

When she was small, her parents never told her that they watched West television. Everybody did but no one liked to admit it. She remembers when she visited a friend; she watched the Sandman on the television and didn't believe that it was the Western Sandman. "We never watch West television, that's my Eastern Sandman," she had stubbornly maintained.

'That was so embarrassing. In this respect my parents were always a bit over-anxious. They could have spared me that embarrassment.'

The bell rings three times. 'Finally, Mutti's here.' Sabine yanks the door open. Her parents are standing before her.

"How come you came home together? You don't come the same way."

"Sometimes we do." Frau Dehnert laughs and hugs her daughter. "Now, are you feeling better? You look chic."

They have forgotten Herr Dehnert again. Sabine often has the feeling her father is not there at all, with his silent manner.

"We can eat straight away." She urges her parents into the sitting room.

"Actually I'm not hungry. The day was really too exciting," Sabine hears her mother say.

"Do come on," she calls impatiently.

When her parents are in the sitting room, Herr Dehnert discovers the parcel at once. He only says, "Mario."

It is endlessly silent in the room but for Sabine the heavy silence lasts too long.

"We're not celebrating Christmas. Come on, let's open the parcel."

She loosens the string.

"Read the address first," asks Frau Dehnert. "Mario Dehnert, Akazienweg 10, So he's living in Hamburg. Isn't there a letter?"

Silently Sabine hands it to her mother.

"Let Vati read the letter, I think he is the calmest of us all. I must sit down first."

Herr Dehnert opens the letter laboriously, clears his throat, and remarking "I've got a frog in my throat," begins to read.

"My dear parents, dear little sister, first the most important thing: I am well. I am unbelievably sorry for all the worries I have caused you in the last weeks. But I was afraid that if I called you and heard your voices, I would change my mind about staying in Hamburg. Yes, I've decided to stay in the West for good. I see no chance back home in the DDR of organising my life as I want to. You know about the difficulties I had in school and that I couldn't get into the EOS* because I wasn't considered politically reliable. The reason was that I let it be known that I didn't want to serve in the National People's Army. In the end I did join. After school nothing was fun for me any more. Not the job training and certainly not the army. The feeling of being shut in depressed me more and more. The two weeks a year in Hungary as compensation only made it worse. I wanted to get out of the stinking DDR and that didn't necessarily mean to the Golden West. Yet there was no other possibility. Where else should I have gone? I simply had had enough of my life being controlled from the cradle to the grave. How I would have loved a year out – to have taken casual work, travelled, played the guitar. But in our Republic, not to want to work is a crime against the state. Here in the West it's all different. That doesn't mean everything is better.

---

* The Sixth Form, years 11 and 12.

38

As you can imagine, the escape was arranged with Aunt Gerda."

Here, Frau Dehnert, startled, interrupts her husband.

"Sabine, did the parcel arrive unopened?"

"Mutti, calm yourself – it arrived in perfect condition."

Herr Dehnert reads on:

"Aunt Gerda was not enthusiastic about my plans. I sent a letter to her from Leipzig via a colleague. I simply said that I already had work prospects in Hamburg and that you agreed with everything, but she shouldn't talk about it over the phone. So that's how it worked out. I picked up my 'welcome money' in Hamburg and then straight away I looked around for work. Relatively soon, I got a temporary job at a petrol station. I don't want to moan, but the work is hard. We do shift work around the clock. There are only foreigners working with me, two Turks, witty guys. We often discuss the wall. They simply can't understand why we Germans didn't rebel against the wall. They reckon that the same thing would be almost inconceivable in Turkey. A wall cutting through an entire country. Neither does the French student, who has the same shift as me, understand the Germans. "Where is your heart?" he always says and grabs his heart in a theatrical way. They all find me exotic. My Saxon accent is a great joke. I only need to open my mouth to get tips -maybe I should join the circus. They certainly have strange ideas about the DDR. My boss thinks the DDR is one big prison. On the other hand his son says that a state in which there are first class athletes and no unemployment can't be so bad; after all, what does one have from the freedom to travel without the money? Then, without drawing breath, he tells me that he's flying to the USA next week for two months and that it's not really so expensive. I turned away without a word and served the next customer. Last week my Turkish mate, Mehmet, invited me home, quite spontaneously. Initially I felt that he wanted to set me up with his pretty daughter but then it turned out to be a nice evening. Mehmet's wife could absolutely not understand why I had left you, seeing there's work over there. "Mario", she said to me, "We only came to Germany because of bread and work. In Turkey there is a lot of hunger. Family must always stay together." She really badgered me. At the end she gave me a packet of Turkish tea for you. The next morning Mehmet asked me straight away whether I had written to you. So I showed him the first page of my letter to you. Mehmet, beaming, took the letter in his hand, held it up the wrong way and winked at me saying, "I can't read!" Then we both laughed so much that our boss came and wanted to know if we were drunk. Mehmet turned round slowly to him and said, "Germans no fun, only work." "In Turkey only fun and no work," retorted my boss. One has to hear these sayings at least twice a day.

So now the best news, I've had a flat for two days now -one bedroom, kitchen and bathroom. It's tiny and only has stove heating but at least I can afford it. I have had such luck. The flat belonged to a regular customer from the filling station. He's moving to Frankfurt. As he also comes from 'over there' – he offered me the flat.

"We have to help you people out," he said. I'm getting a phone next week, then I'll phone you straight away. I often think about you - whether it was the right decision to go away - only the future can show that. I only know that I couldn't go on the way it was. You are in my thoughts – I am really homesick, Your Mario."

Herr Dehnert lets the letter fall. It is completely still – each of them sits lost in thought, in their own corner. In the meantime it has become dark in the sitting room. From outside can be heard the low hooting of cars. The tram rattles past; the usual evening sounds. Together with that can be heard the voices from the TV of the next-door neighbours. 'The West news,' thinks Sabine. 'It's 8 o'clock' She almost envies the neighbours who are watching the news punctually, as they do every evening.

"What do you say to Mario's letter?" Sabine tries to break the silence. Energetically she flicks on the standard lamp.

"I think our Mario has become an adult." Herr Dehnert speaks so quietly that Sabine gets the feeling he is talking to himself. This sentence seems to give life to Frau Dehnert.

"Adult? He is having a bad time. From the first to the last line in the letter, I feel it – I must visit him." She sits upright in her armchair.

"How?" Sabine thinks Mutti is overreacting again.

"Oh, you don't know yet, from the first of the month I'll be in early retirement and so I can travel to the West."

"Oh, that's why I couldn't reach you this afternoon".

"Yes, I took a day off when I found out about it. I picked Vati up and we went for a walk. I had to come to terms with being retired."

"But you wanted to retire."

"Yes, naturally, but first it will be rather strange, without work – but now I must look after Mario."

"What does that mean?" asks Sabine and looks at Vati. He begins to unpack the parcel hesitantly – suddenly he pauses: "Christa, does that mean that you want to leave us too? "

"What do you mean, leave? I want to go and see to Mario. Just understand that I won't have a moment's peace until I know how he lives, what kind of flat he has, whether he is well."

"But you will come back?"

"Well I should hope so," says Sabine.

"Look at everything Mario has sent us," says Frau Dehnert.

Chapter 8

The next weeks flash past. Sabine's thoughts are occupied with the approaching Abitur. Frau Müller leaves the class in peace to a great extent. However there is a small clash over Sabine's West calendar. Completely lost in thought she left an old pocket calendar from the Federal Republic, which she uses as a notebook, lying on her school desk. By chance Frau Müller is standing next to her and sees a bright yellow, eye-catching advertisement for a West German bank on the calendar. Sabine foresees trouble and tries to hide it without attracting attention. But the teacher is quicker. With the words, "Ranzenkontrolle* ought to be enforced at your age, too," she takes the calendar with her to the front of the class.

"How can someone be so stupid," whispers Karin to Sabine. The others appear to feel the same; Renate

---

* Against pornographic and trashy literature. It took place at sporadic intervals, particularly in the case of the younger pupils. The satchels had to be completely emptied. Western publications were confiscated.

43

rolls her eyes and shakes her head. Sabine has gone bright red.

With the remark, "Has your brother already sent you advertising material?" Frau Müller places the calendar in her briefcase.

Despite this unpleasant incident Sabine's Abitur exams go smoothly. Like the other fellow pupils she also receives good results.

"Good Abitur results improve the statistics," criticises Herr Dehnert, "Not that I begrudge you them, Sabine. But it is always the same, we don't get bad results."

Sabine doesn't care. The main thing is that her school time is definitely over.

In high spirits she celebrates with her fellow students. First she can simply enjoy the summer. In autumn she will start the unpopular teacher training. This decision was already made in class eight. Teachers were needed, so one had to fall into line. But at first Sabine had not complied. She had desperately fought for another course of study. She had wanted to study Psychology or unusual languages, such as Japanese.

Her parents had supported her wishes, but at school they fell on deaf ears. Teaching and nothing else. Anger but also desperation made Sabine ill. She didn't eat any more, lost weight quickly, suffered from insomnia and was always unhappy. Her father's most exciting novels didn't take her mind off it, her mother's cakes remained untouched and the West chocolate organised by Mario did not help. After many weeks she was ready to go back to school, unenthusiastically. She was only comforted by the fact that many others in her class were not allowed to study what they wanted either.

But today Sabine isn't thinking about it. She has her first meeting with Thomas in the EisCafe Pinguin.

'What shall I wear? Actually I don't even need to think about it: jeans, a t-shirt, trainers. The standard clothes of our group.'

Thomas, grinning, also notices that, when she arrives intentionally ten minutes late at the EisCafe. With the remark, "There's only a plastic bag missing," he shakes her hand.

"You're not dressed so originally yourself, all in black, in the heat," retorts Sabine.

It's true Thomas is dressed in black from head to toe. Around his neck he is wearing a leather choker with a large wooden cross. However his beaming face is in complete contrast to his gloomy clothes.

"I wear the clothes that I like, and I can annoy a lot of people with the cross. Are you happy now? Come on, let's celebrate your Abi. I'll order us something good, 'Blue Hour', that's a cocktail."

Sabine would like to have eaten an ice cream but a cocktail in the early afternoon seems unusually grown up. The 'Blue Hour' tastes wonderfully sharp and sweet. Sabine thinks Thomas has style. When he wants to know what she is doing in her holidays, she shrugs her shoulders casually and says "Rügen, Bulgaria, Hungary, I'll have see where I want to go this year."

Thomas grins, "Perhaps Italy, or Paris too."

"No, I prefer New York because of the skyscrapers."

"With the choice we have, I can never decide. That's why I always travel to the Müritz-See!"

They both laugh.

"Do you want to come with me?"

"You've got a holiday house, have you?"

"My grandparents."

"Are they nice?"

"The best in the world." Thomas suddenly seems very serious.

"And your parents?" asks Sabine.

"My mum is ok- a bit hectic, but we get on pretty well with each other."

"And your father?" asks Sabine

"I also have a sweet ten-year old sister, Julchen. She's the only committed Communist in our family. She collects old papers, bottles and glass with enthusiasm"*. Apart from that she's the swimming star at the young Pioneers**. She should be sponsored, but my mum, who is a doctor, has forbidden it. It would be too unhealthy. So naturally Julchen is cross."

Sabine, who is dizzy from the cocktail, is not really listening.

"Why doesn't he answer my question about his father, the unfriendly bloke?" She is annoyed.

---

* Because of the shortage of raw materials in the DDR, these resources were collected and recycling was conducted earlier and was more efficient than in most western industrial states. The children donated the proceeds of such actions to charities in the hope that it would help children in the 3rd world.

** Young Pioneers: the children's organisation of the Free German Youth (FDJ).

"And your father?" She doesn't let go.

Thomas is silent, they are both silent.

Sabine has understood; nothing is going to be said about his father. Thomas gets up. "Shall we go for a walk in the Clara-Zetkin Park?"

"I think I need your help to get up, I'm so dizzy. I shouldn't have drunk that second cocktail." Lightly swaying, Sabine gets to her feet and holds on to Thomas.

"Tell me, have you never drunk alcohol, before?"

"Only a glass of Rotkäppchen* at New Year", comes the pathetic reply.

"Are you hungry, do you want a Frankfurter?"

"I'd prefer dry bread. I feel sick."

"Look, my grandparents live nearby. I'll take you there. We can make sandwiches and you can lie down."

Sabine accepts the suggestion gratefully.

---

* A brand of sparkling wine in the DDR.

Chapter 9

'Where am I? How come I'm lying here on this couch?'

Sabine tries to recognise the surrounding noises. Crockery clatters, piano music sounds softly in her ears. There is a wonderful smell of fried potatoes with onions. 'Oh my goodness, I'm at Thomas' grandparents' house.'

The door is carefully opened.

"Are you feeling better?" asks a soft voice.

"Yes."

"I'm Juliane."

"Ah, Julchen."

"I said Juliane!"

The door is slammed shut. Sabine is alone again.

'They're all pig-headed in this family,' thinks Sabine. She hears the little sister calling angrily, "Thomas – why does your friend call me Julchen? Haven't I told you a thousand times …?" The end of the sentence is lost in laughter.

"Don't tickle me!"

The door is roughly thrown open. Julchen and Thomas are standing in the doorway. "Get up, we're eating soon." Thomas laughs at her.

When Sabine enters the living room, there is nobody there.

"We're in the kitchen," calls a strange voice.

She enters, embarrassed.

A small, plump old man with shining eyes, just like Thomas's, gives her his hand.

"I am Herr Reuter, the grandfather, come and sit with us."

A delicate old lady enters, their grandmother. She is very elegantly dressed and has wonderful white hair.

"Welcome to our home, Sabine. Congratulations for passing your Abitur. If only Thomas had got that far".

"It's such a shame that I don't have any grandparents anymore. It's really cosy here."

"And I'm Juliane," says Juliane, irrelevantly.

Everyone laughs. Julchen taps her forehead with her finger and rolls her eyes. Her little blond ponytail flicks to the side. She has tied her Pioneer scarf tightly under her neck.

The meal is fairly chaotic. Everybody talks all at once, but Sabine has the feeling that, despite this, they are all listening to one another.

Thomas reads aloud the holiday postcard from his mother in Bulgaria. The remark: "In swimming costumes we are all the same, East and West," makes everyone laugh.

"Isn't there any dessert?" Julchen's voice is not to be ignored.

The grandfather laughs mischievously.

"I've brought you something back from Frankfurt," and he turns to Sabine. "Frankfurt am Main. I've just got back from there today. I've been a pensioner for a long time," he adds almost apologetically.

"Chocolates!" Julchen shrieks with delight.

"They're not for you, they're from our class enemy." Thomas lovingly tugs his sister's Pioneer scarf.

"Beast." As quick as lightning she snatches a chocolate. Still chewing, she explains to Sabine. "Grandpa is the best smuggler. He smuggles valuable stamps over the border for an old friend, and sells them in the West."

"There were only two," interjects the Grandfather, laughing.

"Do you know where he hid them? In a packet of tissues." Julchen quickly puts a chocolate in her mouth.

"With the money he gets, Grandpa buys not only chocolate but also…" Thomas leans close to Sabine's ear. "The best books, which are forbidden over here. Julchen mustn't know. She is capable of telling someone. We already have a veritable lending library. Lots of friends want to read the books."

Sabine is amazed and thinks that her parents would never dare to do something like that.

"How did you like Frankfurt?"

"Do you know Sabine, that is not easy to explain. For us old people it's too hectic over there. The traffic is extremely dangerous, the shops have such a range of goods for sale that it makes you quite dizzy. And then the prices. Imagine, I saw five different prices for butter. One always has to compare them, which

50

is very tiring. Luckily books and newspapers cost the same everywhere, which is the most important thing for me. In Frankfurt I spent the whole day reading in the library. You know Sabine, books are my life."

"I almost forgot!" Thomas gets up and gets a parcel out of the cupboard. "Here is my present for you for passing the Abitur."

Sabine promptly goes bright red. "Damn, why does that have to happen to me now?" she thinks.

"Open it", urges Julchen

A bright yellow scarf appears, and wrapped in it, a small book, 'Greece and its Islands'. "You love foreign countries, perhaps you'll get there one day." Thomas is a bit embarrassed

"Thank you," stutters Sabine, confused. Suddenly she begins to cry.

"Sorry, you must have an awful impression of me."

The grandmother looks a little astonished. Julchen hands her a handkerchief.

"It's just that it's my first present since the Abitur. My parents are in such a state that they haven't got a moment to think about me. Weeks ago I applied for a visa for all of us to Hungary; we wanted to go there after my Abitur. Now nothing's going to come of it. No one wants to come with me. What am I supposed to do alone in Hungary?" Sabine sobs.

"Such a cry-baby, first drinks cocktails and then blubbers," Julchen interjects.

"Juliane be quiet." The grandmother is angry. She puts her arm round Sabine's shoulders.

"Parents have their own worries too, so children have to take second place at times." "Oh", Sabine blows her nose. "They're my worries too. But please don't tell anyone else about this." Sabine thinks of Julchen's quick tongue, but she has left the room in a sulk.

"My brother went to the West. To Hamburg, forever. Mutti is very worried about him. But Mario's over twenty! Today Mutti went there. She's been an early pensioner since the first of the month. I, I'm so worried that she…" Sabine stops mid-sentence.

"I can't bring myself to say it."

She feels the grandmother gently stroking her back.

"You're afraid that your mother will stay in Hamburg, too." Thomas's reply is barely audible and he seems terribly sad. "Just like my father five years ago."

"Oh, children, it really is much too difficult for you. Making decisions like this puts immeasurable strain on all of us. We cannot accept that they go, even though we always want the best for our children. Sabine, I was desperate when our son, our only child, stayed in the West on a business trip. Still, we must not blame those who go. Above all we should blame those who tolerated this state of affairs." Her voice becomes firm again. "We must not give up on ourselves. In our country something must change, and soon."

"But we have to do something to make that happen," Thomas's voice sounds uncertain.

"We certainly must, my boy," replies the grandfather. "Perhaps we should take Sabine home first though. It is already dark. I suggest we all accompany her together."

Despite the warm summer evening there are only a few people on the streets. Several youths are lounging on the park bench, drinking beer.

"Nothing ever happens here, everyone just sits in front of the TV and watches West TV, every evening." Thomas is getting annoyed. "Sabine, do you want to go to Kulkwitzer Lake tomorrow for a swim?"

"Only if everyone comes too." This evening she feels more protected than she has for a long time.

Chapter 10

Sabine and her father are sitting silently at the breakfast table. A letter from Frau Dehnert has just arrived from Hamburg.

"Mutti could have phoned us! Especially as we've been waiting so long for news." Sabine spreads her bread and tries to stay calm. "I simply don't understand Mutti. Mario is really old enough to manage alone. She's not thinking about us at all."

"Don't speak like that about your mother," Herr Dehnert wants to get up but Sabine holds on to his arm firmly.

"Is that your only comment? Aren't you going to say anything about the fact that our family practically doesn't exist?" Sabine's voice cracks.

Helplessly, Herr Dehnert strokes his daughter's hair. "Calm yourself, child. Mutti writes that she is only staying with Mario for as long as he needs her help."

"Do you really believe that? We know so many people who have not returned."

"But Sabine, Mutti didn't leave illegally, she is a pensioner. She won't get any peace until she has seen with her own eyes that Mario's OK. So for the moment we must show some understanding. Look, here's a suggestion. Put in an application for a travel permit for the West to join your mother. I'm sure you'll get permission. The requirements are supposed to have been relaxed."

Sabine finds the calm way in which her father deals with the situation almost uncanny. He is probably more deeply affected than he wants to admit. Her father has a constant stomach-ache and is now taking a pill.

"Oh, Vati, you're always so understanding of other people. Sorry about just now." Shyly, she gives him a kiss on his cheek. Tender gestures are unusual in their family.

"Do you know, Sabine, perhaps you can take care of the housekeeping. I'll take over at the weekend. Tell me, if you need money." Herr Dehnert turns to leave, but remains standing for a while. "Sabine, don't worry so much. Look, Mutti and Mario are together in Hamburg. Perhaps Mutti can fulfil her dream and travel with her friend, Gisela, to the Mediterranean. She lives near Hamburg. I'm sure they've already made plans, especially as Gisela gets a good pension. We're going to get along alone well for a while, don't you think? We're not living in normal times. The circumstances in our country are splitting up a lot of families. We're not the only ones. Something is bound to change. Now that Gorbachov is here. On West TV they even talked about reducing travel restrictions."

Herr Dehnert leaves the flat. Sabine watches him, hidden behind the net curtain. Her father seems smaller and more bent than normal. He seems not to notice a neighbour who goes by, greeting him.

"What is going to become of us?" ponders Sabine. "Perhaps I really should apply for a travel permit. Then I can tell Mummy off. After all, in our family not everyone can one do what they want."

Sabine thinks of Thomas and his grandparents. She liked the atmosphere there, relaxed and jolly.

'My parents always seem somehow depressed and also discontented,' she thinks. 'If I'm honest, I couldn't speak to Mario at all. He was always crazy about the West; otherwise he wasn't much interested in anything. He just wanted to go. The environmental group was something that was purely a waste of time for him.' The parents were also unenthusiastic about her group, they were afraid that she was doing something illegal. What had Thomas's grandfather read on a wall in Frankfurt? 'Those who don't resist live wrongly'. 'We could impress that upon ourselves here.' Sabine eats her third bread roll, completely lost in thought. 'At home they moan about that sort of thing. They don't protest at school or at work. At the obligatory celebrations for the Republic they wave their little flags, after that they go to the Intershop and squander their West money.' Sabine thinks that she has the right viewpoint.

When, two hours later, whilst swimming, she puts her thoughts to Thomas, he only says, "You're very self-righteous. What does it mean, to resist? My grandfather has always resisted; where has that got him? They took the directorship in the company away from him, later they limited his pension to the minimum. Colleagues were afraid to have contact with him. He managed to feed his family with small commissions. My grandmother is a painter, but her paintings were too negative. Suddenly she didn't get any more commissions, neither did her paintings sell any more. Who wanted paintings by a painter who had fallen into disgrace hanging in their flat? So until her pension she worked in the museum as a guard."

"Do you think that they both regret it?" Sabine looks at Thomas questioningly.

"No, absolutely not. But for my father, his parents' attitude was difficult. He knew that they also wanted a decision from him. So he chose to stay in the West at the first opportunity. You can't demand that much courage from everybody," Thomas says pensively.

"Come on, Sabine don't take everything so seriously. A new life is beginning for you. Studying. Marvellous. You're in a much better situation than I am. I still have a year until my Abitur, then I'll go into the army. Perhaps I'll be stationed somewhere on the border. Do you know what that means? Watch out that no one escapes from our beloved Republic. But going to the Bausoldaten* won't help either. The best thing would be to refuse completely, but then that would definitely mean prison.

---

* The possibility existed in the DDR - albeit limited to very small numbers - to serve without taking up arms, in the so-called Builders' Unit, building military installations. However, refusal to do active military service would create huge hurdles in the path to one's future progress, for example for one's studies.

My family would understand, but I simply could not put them through that."

"Me neither," Sabine replies abruptly. She jumps up, and running quickly to the lake, she throws herself into the waves.

Chapter 11

Tired, but at last a little more contented and confident, Sabine goes home. It is Thursday afternoon; her father has gone to stay with a friend for a few days. Sabine had advised him to do so, he looked so pale and tired. Both of them want to go hiking. She is looking forward to having the flat to herself.

She goes into the kitchen, her stomach grumbling violently.

When she has made fried eggs and bacon, is laying the table and thinking about turning on the TV, it occurs to her that she has not yet seen the post. Her curiosity is stronger than her hunger. Although the meal is already on the table, Sabine runs quickly to the post-box on the ground floor.

An official letter from Berlin is the only post. "Surely this is my permission to visit Mummy, now I can get going."

Happily she climbs the stairs, two at a time. Whilst eating she opens the letter. Sabine cannot believe her eyes. Her application has been rejected, without a statement detailing any reasons. Days later she will learn, on the grapevine, the reasons for her rejection. Because her brother has left the DDR illegally, she is not allowed to visit her mother.

Sabine's world falls apart.

"When will I next see Mutti, or Mario? What am I doing here, in a country which won't allow me to see my mother for just one week? We're not criminals. If only Vati were here, or Thomas. Why doesn't he have a telephone?" Sabine paces up and down nervously in the flat. She switches on the TV, because she can't bear the silence all around her. The West news has already begun. She only listens with half an ear. Suddenly Sabine stares at the screen intently. The newsreader comments on the picture shown. "With the toleration of the Hungarian government and the help of the Red Cross, a hundred-and-eight DDR citizens, who were staying in the West German Embassy in Budapest, were allowed via Vienna into the Federal Republic. More and more DDR citizens are succeeding in their escape to the West over the green border from Hungary to Austria. In the meantime, their number stands at around 3000."

A young reporter appears on the screen. The background is full of people. "Many DDR citizens have used their holiday to Hungary to leave the DDR. They have brought only what is most necessary. Luckily the nights are still warm, so that no one has to freeze at night.

Furthermore, hundreds of DDR citizens are squeezing themselves into the West German Embassy, living in the smallest of spaces. The sanitary conditions are catastrophic. The people seem sad and depressed.

Many are sleeping in their cars in the area surrounding the embassy. All hope to obtain permission to get out to the Federal Republic. The Hungarian government has promised the refugees that none of them will be sent back to the DDR."

'The ones who are leaving are still quite young,' thinks Sabine. 'Lots of them are my age.'

She spends the whole evening watching lots of special programmes about the constantly growing influx of refugees.

DDR citizens are also waiting for their departure at the German Embassy in Prague. When asked about the reasons for their flight, they all say the same: "We want freedom – you only live once – We want to be able to travel unhindered. – We're doing it for our children - It's getting better everywhere in the East, only back home it's getting worse."

After that, young people who are being helped by the Red Cross are interviewed. Sabine stares at the screen.

'The young people actually look quite happy,' she thinks. 'With their rucksacks, they look more like tourists who have been on a night- time hike. Not at all like refugees.'

Champagne bottles are being passed around. Words such as 'crazy, inconceivable, indescribable' are being constantly repeated. Tears flow, whether from grief, fury, joy or relief, one cannot tell.

A young girl is asked whether her parents knew that she had escaped.

"No, of course not. But my mother lives in Stuttgart, I want to go there too. No power on Earth will stop me."

She laughs into the camera, and makes the victory sign with two fingers of her right hand. It seems to Sabine that she is winking at her, and saying, "Come with us. Who knows when there will be such a chance again?" As if the television commentator has been listening to their secret dialogue, he points out that it is feared that the DDR government will close the borders, and not issue visas any more. Sabine jumps up from her chair, as if electrocuted.

'I must make inquiries at once about my Hungarian visa. It should have arrived ages ago. I've had enough. I want to go too. Perhaps this is the last chance to get out.'

She hardly sleeps that night. Again and again she gets up and searches for forgotten pieces of memorabilia, tries out sturdy shoes, sorts out photos, gathers her documents together. She wants to take as little as possible with her.

Then she makes a list of all the things she needs to do.

'Most importantly I need to withdraw money from my savings bank. Where can my rucksack be? In the attic probably. Tomorrow I'll buy a film to take photos of my certificates. I'll leave the film in the camera. At a checkpoint the school documents would arouse suspicion.'

Sabine has everything worked out in her mind. She knows that next week Thomas' best friend is going to Budapest to meet his girlfriend from Cologne. He can easily take her with him in his car. As far as Budapest, after that she must go on alone.

Chapter 12

Sabine experiences the next days as if she is in a dream. Everything seems so unreal, as if it is not she who is making the decisions, preparing for her departure. Everything goes like clockwork, like in a dream. Sabine receives her visa for Hungary punctually. Getting a lift with Wolfgang, Thomas's friend, is no problem; she finds her rucksack.

Sabine lays the things she wants to take with her on the table. It is not a lot: a camera with a film - she has photographed her documents - underwear, money, travel papers, jumper, jacket, socks, sandwiches, swimming costume - it should look as if she is going on holiday - photos of her parents and of friends. In the scarf from Thomas she wraps a small bottle of perfume.

She locks childhood memories, letters and a lot of other things in a chest, which she stows under her bed. She leaves a letter for her father on the kitchen table. She found this letter of departure really difficult to write. Especially as she had felt lately that she had got closer to her father, understood him better.

'Despite this there is nothing to stop me.'

Stop, she has forgotten something. The book from Thomas: 'Greece and its Islands.' Together they have looked at all the islands on the map and dreamed of going there. "What is so normal for Tanja is forbidden for us, why?" she said bitterly to Thomas. Thomas tried to comfort her. He said not all young people in the West had the money to go on such a trip either.

"I've heard it's cheaper than our Bulgarian trip last year. Never again! How we were treated there. Not only the fact that we all got the same meals in the restaurants and the hotels were worse than those of the West Germans, at the airport there were two different waiting lounges as well. As we took off, all the planes were greatly delayed. It was disgustingly humid. Imagine, the West Germans could buy themselves juice, we couldn't. Because we had no Deutschmarks. Never again for me."

Thomas laughed and pointed on the map to a Greek island. "When you swim in that sea for the first time, you'll forget all this."

Had he already guessed then that she would leave? In any case he wasn't especially surprised when Sabine told him of her decision. Naturally she asked him whether he wanted to come with her. He didn't even reply to that. Despite this she didn't have the feeling that he was angry. Only very sad, but she was as well.

' It's strange. I have the feeling that Thomas gave me the strength to go. He and his grandparents. They accepted my plans. However, the grandparents worried too much about how I was going to get over the border.

As I didn't know it myself, I simply said my mother was waiting for me in Budapest.'

Sabine's travel preparations were not noticed by anybody else. Almost all her friends were away. Moreover, in August 1989 the people were so preoccupied with themselves that Sabine's behaviour did not attract attention. Whether to go or to stay - this question concerns many people.

The number of DDR refugees who are trying to get into the Federal Republic via Czechoslovakia, Poland or Hungary is rising every day.

Sabine has the feeling that the whole of the DDR is leaving. Only the government is acting as if nothing is happening. The gaps which the people have left behind are obvious. When Sabine wants to buy bread for the journey from the baker, the shop is 'closed for the time being'. The pub on the corner always has 'day off' and the children's doctor has been on holiday for weeks.

Sabine cannot get rid of the feeling that her house is also getting emptier from day to day.

'It's time that I left,' she tries to convince herself.

When the time actually comes she can hardly grasp it. The farewell from Thomas is cool; neither wants to show their feelings in front of the other.

"Write, won't you", says Thomas.

"Get in touch", answers Sabine.

"I haven't got your address."

"Here's Mario's." Sabine hands him a piece of paper from her pocket, with the address already on it She gets into Wolfgang's Trabi quickly. The farewell of the two friends, even when only for three weeks, seems profoundly warmer.

It lasts too long for her anyway. When Wolfgang finally gets in behind the steering wheel, she grumpily says to him, "About time."

"You can't get away from us fast enough. By the way, we're going to stop in Dresden quickly. I have to pick up a spare tyre from a friend. We didn't have any."

Sabine conceals her annoyance and looks out of the window. The streets in the suburbs are empty, only a few older people can be seen. A queue has formed in front of the greengrocer's.

"Probably grapes, they had them there yesterday, anyway," says Wolfgang and offers Sabine one. "Tell me, why do you actually want to go?"

"Oh, so much has happened to me recently." Sabine looks out of the window. "I've just got the feeling, if I don't leave, I won't ever have the chance again to live how I want."

They are soon in Dresden. Wolfgang's friend calls after Sabine: "Don't forget us, don't forget the ones who are staying!"

They soon reach the Czechoslovakian border too. They drive through the whole night, only taking short breaks to sleep.

Both of them want to be in Hungary as quickly as possible.

"Who knows whether the border is actually still open for us?"

In the morning they reach the Hungarian border. Friendly officials let them through. They could be a young couple going on holiday.

It is a wonderful summer's day, nobody seems to be thinking of escaping. Sabine winds down the window. "Here, you can really breathe deeply."

"Just wait," says Wolfgang ironically, "Perhaps you'll miss our Leipzig air one day."

Sabine is quite lost in thought. ' What will I do if I don't like it over there?'

Her eyes flood with tears. The relief of having left the DDR gives way to a feeling of sadness.

'How should I organise the escape? I should have let Mutti know.'

As if Wolfgang had guessed her thoughts he says, "When we're in Budapest, we'll look for a guest house, where you can call your mum from. Tell me, is she still in Hamburg or might she have gone to Leipzig? That could be possible, couldn't it?"

"Are you mad? Well actually, I had already thought of that," Sabine admits in a subdued manner.

"You know, my girlfriend can find out for you how the others are managing to get across the border. As a West German she won't arouse suspicion."

"She'll thank you for that! It's your holiday. Where are you actually meeting her?"

"At four o'clock in our usual café." Wolfgang seems quite nervous.

"Don't you want to go over with your girlfriend?"

"I have thought about it. But it's not that serious with Inge yet. And I don't know anyone over there either. In the end I would just live at her expense." Wolfgang smiles at Sabine, embarrassed.

Inge is waiting at the agreed place, she has already organised accommodation. Straight away Sabine calls Hamburg from the guest house. When she hears her mother's voice she has to sit down because she is so excited, her legs are trembling. She hears her mother's amazed reply, "Child, where are you? I've been ringing Leipzig so often."

Sabine can only say quietly, "I'm in Budapest and I want to come to you."

"My darling." The warmth which radiates from her mother's voice seems to have a calming effect on Sabine. "Have you thought about it properly?"

"I want to come to you." Sabine can say nothing else.

"Then come, I'm waiting for you," replies her mother calmly but determinedly. "If only I could help you! Should I come?"

"No, it's too late now. I'll call you when I…no you know already. Not over the phone." Sabine suddenly has an uneasy feeling as the owner of the guesthouse enters the hall.

'After all, who knows if she'll report me to the police.' She darts quickly into her room.

Next morning she goes with Inge and Wolfgang to the German Embassy. It is like a besieged fortress. Everywhere there are groups standing together, talking. Children are playing, a few are crying. There is so little room that one can hardly move. Many have stayed the night in tents in the embassy gardens. In the meantime it has become cool and rainy. A tense atmosphere prevails. The people are on edge.

'There's no way I'm staying here,' thinks Sabine, distressed.

Rumours circulate that the refugees have to return to the DDR.

Many young people feel dejected owing to the fact that they have not told their parents of their escape.

Two young girls from Schwerin tell Sabine that they persuaded a cameraman from the 'West news' to film them for the evening news. Now they are hoping that their parents will see them on television and so feel calmer.

Inge has very quickly found out where it is possible to cross the border with relatively little danger. It is favourable, too, that the crossing place from Budapest is easy to reach. Sabine wants to attempt the escape that night.

"Come on, Sabine, let's stroll around for a bit," suggests Inge. "You still have time. It must get dark first. We'll drive you to the border. I invite you all to dinner."

'Inge is enviable,' thinks Sabine. 'She's so self-confident. She's so sure of herself in a foreign country.'

Finally, after a long search they buy a pocket torch and a compass for the escape. Inge gives Sabine her raincoat.

Together they mark on the map where she must cross the border. Inge describes to her how the border fences must look, what she must look out for. She got the information from a couple who want to go over the border at this spot the next day.

When they reach the small village at the border at about eight pm, they see countless Trabis which have been dismantled, standing along the village street. Their owners have probably been in the West for a long time.

In the village pub they drink a coke. Apart from two youths they are the only customers.

'They're from the East too,' thinks Sabine.

They get talking. Quickly it turns out that they both want to use the same escape route. They have both tried it at another spot twice already, in vain Jürgen and Stefan, as they are called, persuade Sabine to go with them.

In the meantime it has become pitch black. Sabine becomes uneasy. Inge and Wolfgang promise her that they will wait two hours, in case she is brought back by the border guards.

"Nothing much can happen." Sabine tries to reassure herself. "Go on you two. Show me the way." She tries to make her voice sound firm.

In silence the three make their way into an unknown land.

Chapter 13

At some stage Sabine fell asleep, exhausted, on the raised hunters' hideout.

Dream and reality merge into each other. Suddenly she is roughly shaken awake. She has trouble getting her bearings.

"It's already light. Do you want the border soldiers to get us? Get up, Sabine!" Stefan is standing in front of her. Suddenly she is awake.

"It's true - I didn't just dream all of that, I really am escaping."

Sabine carefully climbs down the raised tower. All her bones are aching. She is unaccustomed to sleeping in an upright position.

"Where are we?" Jürgen and Stefan look at her questioningly.

"I have no idea."

The three roam about, lost, and stop and look at each other helplessly. They don't know what to do next. Suddenly Jürgen says, "Look, there's something over there on the tree, perhaps…" Jürgen does not go on, as if afraid to get anyone's hopes up.

As they get nearer they see that there is a wooden plaque fixed on the tree, *'In memory of the seven hikers who were struck by lightening at this place on 24th September 1951.'*

Sabine reads the words on the plaque aloud very slowly. "Oh my goodness, that's in German!" She calls out. "We've made it!"

The three embrace each other. They have tears in their eyes.

"Yes, we've done it."

Sabine cries unashamedly. Jürgen looks at her and says in a hoarse voice, "We've managed the first step, but the most difficult part is still ahead. Will we find a new home there? I'm homesick already."

Chapter 14

Hamburg, 20th September 1989

Dear Thomas,
You must think I'm an unfaithful friend, because apart from a postcard you haven't had one sign of life from me. But you've been pretty lazy about writing, too. I'm a bit scared, actually, that you've forgotten me. I've been living in Hamburg for just four weeks. It seems as if with each day I know less and less where I belong. Only now do I realise what I have lost: family, friends, Leipzig. Perhaps it sounds a bit theatrical, but read my letter first.

I'm living with Mario. As he only has one room, I sleep in the kitchen on a folding bed. Living together is going well, as Mario's not at home much. When he is there he sits silently in front of the TV. He hasn't changed much. Before he used to moan about the DDR, and now he moans about the BRD. He doesn't want to go back though, most of all he'd like to emigrate, to

Australia. I think he's very homesick, but obviously he would never admit it.

I have the feeling that Mario wanted to get away from the family, and now we're all following him. It didn't go well with Mutti at all. Her constant bossiness got on his nerves. When she started to furnish his flat "cosily" there was a row. Mutti lives outside Hamburg with a friend, who came over here a few years ago.

We phone each other frequently, but meet less often; the train connections aren't particularly good.

Luckily Mutti gets on very well with her friend Gisela; they went to school together. They're both very active and they're constantly going on trips together. No special travel offer is safe from them, and Mario and I are glad that this friend exists, because firstly she satisfies Mutti's desire to travel, and secondly, Mutti doesn't have so much time to fuss over us. However, Mutti's all the more worried about Vati. I think she's got a pretty bad conscience about being here in Hamburg with us and leaving him to cope alone in Leipzig. After all, they had only agreed that she would see to Mario in Hamburg. Naturally my leaving changed everything again. When Vati came back from the hike with his friend and found my letter, he must have been quite desperate. Mutti says that he really feels left in the lurch by all of us. That upsets us a lot. After my successful escape Mutti came to Vienna. A whole lot of formalities had to be dealt with, and then we went to Mario in Hamburg. I got my first welfare payment right away, and that was that. It's strange; you clear off and get

---

BRD Bundesrepublik Deutschland, the former West Germany.

money for it. I'm exaggerating, it wasn't quite that easy. I had to go round all the registration offices. There are an awful lot of them here, from the job centre to the social services to the residents' registration authorities and back to the job centre, and so on. And then all the incomprehensible forms you have to fill in. You're warned again and again to read the small print, it's supposed to be the most important part. I want to know why they can't print it so you don't have to ruin your eyesight reading it, if that's the case.

"You don't have to come here," one of the officials said to me. I went away, bright red in the face. Then a 'resettler' - that's what they call us here - from Dresden, explained everything to me. Just imagine - they didn't accept his diploma. When I asked him why he had left Dresden, he said in his best Saxon, "Didn't want to be inferior any more." I wonder what he makes of that now.

I spent the first two weeks sitting around at home; I didn't really know what to do with myself. Mutti and I constantly thought about what I could do. I didn't want to study to start with, but first to earn some money.

Mutti and I often met up in a café in the town centre, the waitress got to know us. I think she felt sorry for us. She knew I was looking for a job. One day she pointed out an advert in the newspaper; they were looking for untrained helpers in a nursing home. I went straight there the next day, what can I say, they were extremely happy that I'd come.

I have shift work. The old people are nice. They're glad that I come from 'over there', from the 'Ostzone.'

A lot of them were there before the war, in Leipzig or on Rügen.

It's harder with my colleagues, They're always making jokes about the DDR. Although not one of them has been there, they all know better. When I said yesterday, really astonished, to the ward sister, "Oh, there's no company nursery here," she answered snappily, "It's not necessary for mothers to work here. They prefer to look after their children themselves." Just as snappily I replied, "Here the unemployed fathers could look after their children too!" Then there was uproar. Our male nurse butted in right away.

"Sabine, have you ever thought that you've cashed in on our benefits, that you'll probably soon receive our housing allowance? What have you achieved for our state then? Your mother gets our pension, in fact more than my mother. Has your mother worked over here then?" With a bright red face he stood before me. That wasn't the end of it. Our ward helper had her say too:

"Our government ought to forbid the people from the East from coming over here. And the Poles and the Russians too There are supposed to be hundreds of thousands of them. We've already got so many foreigners here."

"But I am German," I let it slip out.

"Let me tell you something," our male nurse butted in again, "You were discontented over there. Now you can't wait to earn money over here. But you have to do something for that. Some of you work at my baker's. He told me yesterday they don't want to work at all. They can't take an eight-hour day; nor do they want to. They have themselves written off as sick. Well, you're not like that. There are always exceptions. But for us you're all foreigners, somehow."

Maria, a young colleague, joins in. I was just about to go, when she said, "Sabine, let them talk. They're only angry because they know that without us foreigners, they would have to close the home. Come on let's dish out the breakfast. We don't have time to gossip. Foreigners prefer to work."

I was speechless. When I wanted to thank Maria, I had to say, however, that I didn't come from Poland, I was German. She just laughed and said: "For the people here you're apparently just as foreign as me!"

When she saw my astonished face, she asked:

"Didn't you know that I'm Greek?"

What do you think of that? She comes from Greece, unfortunately not from an island. We have sort of become friends.

You know, Thomas, that I'm taking something away from others, that really got to me. I really notice how I control myself in the presence of my colleagues. I don't wear my new jumper to work, otherwise they'll be thinking they paid for it. I prefer to keep it quiet that Mutti gave me a ticket for a BAP concert.

I often think of you in Leipzig. Does our environment group still exist?

If only I knew if my decision was right. If they had just given me that visitors' permit, who knows… My father is naturally angry with us. He wrote to me, saying that he's very sad that we all left him alone. He doesn't want us to write to him or phone him at the moment. He'll get in touch when he thinks the time is right. So, a lot has changed in my life. In the daytime there's so much happening to me that I don't have time to think, but at night I suddenly wake up and ponder about what will happen. In Leipzig I somehow lived a more carefree life, and now I have to act like an adult. Oh, Thomas, you wouldn't recognise me any more, I've become so serious. I sometimes feel damned alone and feel quite overcome by all the problems.

I'd be so happy if you would write to me, but in detail, OK?

Don't be surprised if this letter has a Leipzig postmark. My mother's friend is taking it with her tomorrow. After all, this letter should only be read by you. Don't forget me altogether.

Your Sabine.

Sabine does not have to wait long for an answer from Thomas. A letter comes back to her the same way.

Leipzig, 24th Sept 1989

Dear Sabine,

I jumped for joy when I got your letter. I was pretty desperate already. I didn't get any card from you. Opa wanted to go to Hamburg next week and look for you. Renate and Karin are quite annoyed that they haven't heard from you. They were furious when they found out about your 'journey'. I think they miss you. Me too, I wouldn't have thought it.

Julchen is insulted because you didn't say goodbye to her. She wanted to give you a farewell picture. She spent quite a while drawing it. I'm sending it to you. In case you don't recognise it straight away; the two in the picture are us at the EisCafe Pinguin. She says you should come back at once. If not, then she wants a comic book from you. Apparently she collects them, although there aren't any here. On the day I got your letter, our group met up in the afternoon. At least a third has gone, just cleared off. The atmosphere in the group is fittingly depressed. In any case we are going to demonstrate on our anniversary, the 7th October*. It doesn't matter what risks we take. I don't watch the DDR TV programmes any more. They only lie to us. On West TV one only sees the happy faces of people who have succeeded in their escape. I feel like the last Mohican. Anyway our family is staying, to the bitter end. Mutti doesn't want to leave her patients in the lurch. She doesn't want to do it to our grandparents either.

Vati has written again, Granny told me. He also sent a parcel but Mutti is not allowed to know anything about it. Tomorrow we are going to the photographer, Vati is going to get a new photo of us. He writes that he longs to see Julchen and me. I miss him too. He was always so funny and he was good at maths. Do you know Sabine, I would have liked to leave with you, but I didn't have the courage. Incidentally, Wolfgang has not returned from his holiday in Hungary. I feel really alone, just like you. Karin has seen your father. She says that he looks very bad. Your father questioned her thoroughly about you, but she didn't know anything either. All the best, Sabine, don't forget the DDR.

Your Thomas

---

* 40th anniversary of the founding of the DDR

P.S. Your friend is taking this letter with her the day after tomorrow.

Sabine puts down the letter sadly. She looks at Julchen's drawing. That was all such a long time ago, the 'Blue Hour' in the Eiscafe. The picture is a little strange to her. For the first time she feels that there is already a distance between herself and the DDR. Through Maria life has become a little more colourful. Yesterday they went for a stroll through Hamburg's boutiques, went to the cinema and afterwards went to a cosy Greek restaurant. She has since lost a bit of her fear of the city. Most of all, she liked the huge number of music shops. She could stay there for hours on end, listening to music.

She has got to know Maria's family; they are also separated. Two of her brothers live in Greece, Maria and her parents in Hamburg. Their grandmother always travels there and back and is the source of all the latest family gossip.

When Sabine puts the letter back in the envelope again, she discovers that there is a piece of notepaper in it. Astonished, she begins to read it.

Supplement Monday 25th September

Oh, Sabine, I'm still finding it hard to calm down. Just imagine it, today was my first demonstration. There were thousands of us on the streets of Leipzig**. Renate

---

** In Leipzig around 8000 people demonstrated on 25th September 1989 for freedom of opinion and assembly and to demand that the ban against the opposition group, 'Neues Forum', be lifted.

and Karin told me about the demonstration. I just went there and had a look at it, from a distance. I was standing in a crowd of onlookers. The demonstration had come from in front of the Nikolaikirche, where the Peace Prayers took place.

Until then the demonstrators who wanted to leave shouted, "We want to get out!" but today a lot of them called, "We are staying here!" I was a bit scared to join in. There were supposed to have been a lot of informers there. The whole demonstration was escorted by the police. Later they beat up and arrested people without reason. I immediately joined a group of people who were collecting evidence of police interference. Suddenly Renate and Karin went running past me. They called to me, said I should hurry otherwise my life would pass me by. The people laughed, I was a bit embarrassed. Well, then I went with them, or rather, ran with them. I dived into a flowing current and suddenly felt very strong. The demonstrators kept shouting, "Join us!" and then people jumped over the street barriers and ran with them. You couldn't see for the mass of people.

I think that the people of Leipzig showed courage when they went on the streets although nobody could know what would come of it.

Bine, I'm happy. It is as if a veil of mist has been wiped from my face. I suddenly feel free and light. If things here change I want to be a part of it. Every day, every hour. I won't allow myself to miss one minute. Now I am going to live, at last.

Chapter 15

The alarm clock rings relentlessly. It is 6 o'clock. Without turning on the light, Sabine feels for the alarm clock and turns it off.

'I'll give myself ten more minutes. I don't always have to be so super punctual at the ward. Mario has already gone. He's always so considerate in the mornings. After all, I am lying in his kitchen,' she thinks and is quite touched. 'Luckily he can have breakfast at work. Perhaps I should talk to him. He seems so depressed.'

Mario finds no other work than that in the petrol station. Yesterday he said quite sadly, "Now I have the coolest stereo system, better than anything I ever dreamed of, and I am so worn out in the evening that I go to sleep to the loudest music. My brand new guitar stands unused in the corner. I never imagined life in the West to be like this."

Sabine had secretly put in an advert in the Hamburg newspaper; 'Young guitarist seeks a group to make music with.'

She had wanted to write, 'Young guitarist from the DDR', but Maria said, "Then no one will apply. Your taste in music is quite outdated."

That had started the first quarrel between the two friends.

"At least I know who Goethe and Bismarck are, for you they are completely unknown quantities," hissed back Sabine.

The next day Maria brought with her a book by Goethe in Greek and Sabine a tape, 'Rock from the DDR.' Then they both laughed so much that they cried.

Nevertheless, no one replied to the advertisement. She had given Maria's address. Mario was not to know anything about it. He would definitely have been against it. He had inhibitions about the Westerners.

"They're so perfect, in music too, I can't keep up with them in that." That was his opinion.

Sabine forces herself out of bed. While she is sitting in the underground it occurs to her how much she has already got used to her working routine. She wouldn't want to do this forever.

Her wage isn't bad but she finds the shift work very tiring. She is constantly tired and on top of that there are stabbing pains in her back. A colleague showed her how to wash a patient and change the bed without dislocating herself, but in the chaos of the everyday routine she forgets to pay attention to it.

Yesterday an old lady died quite suddenly. Sabine was so shattered that the nurse sent her home.

"That's a lot to cope with, especially for such a young girl as you. After all you have come straight from school to us. Go and relax at home."

Sabine is happy that her colleagues have become considerably more friendly to her. They notice that she's not work shy. "Although she has the Abitur," as one ward helper stresses. 'Strange,' thinks Sabine, 'what plays a role here in the West. If the Abitur is so important here, perhaps I should still study. Perhaps I should build on my Russian as they're all so wild about it in the West since Gorbachov.'

Yesterday a young, fashionably dressed woman sat opposite her in the underground, with a scarf tied around her printed with Russian letters and a hammer and sickle. The really smart people wear the red star on their berets.

'No one would do that at home voluntarily,' thinks Sabine. 'Will I ever be able to stop saying 'at home'? Yesterday Maria asked me how I had imagined the West to be. "Not as loud or brightly coloured." I answered spontaneously. 'Yes, that's right. I'd thought the West was like Budapest, like Hungary, the Caribbean of the East. Lots of cafes, shops, overflowing fruit shops, cinemas that show films from all over the world.

Hungary was the front garden of Paradise for us. I now see that Budapest is a joke compared to Hamburg. Here, I didn't trust myself to go shopping at first. At the butcher's I still can't decide which of the endless types of sausage I should take. In the cheese department I break into a sweat. Because I don't know the names I unfailingly point to the most expensive sort but they just taste so delicious. Maria laughed and said that it was the same for her at the beginning – if only I could be like Maria, so self-confident and assured! I grew up so protected at home. School, the youth organisation, one was part of the collective. One didn't have to decide anything for oneself, it was decided for you.'

When Sabine comes to the ward there is a small surprise waiting for her. For her overtime she receives one hundred marks extra.

'I'll squander this senselessly right away, this afternoon', she thinks, pleased, and dishes out the breakfast. She sees the sisters with sullen faces rush past her.

'Strange people in the West. They seem so discontented. They often talk about money; they always have too little, but look at all the things they can afford! And then all the names; credit, leasing, cheques, credit cards, cash points, shares, insurance and of course debts.'

After work she goes into the town centre straight away. In the grocery of a big department store, she allows herself the luxury of buying all sorts of yoghurt that up until now she didn't know. In the same way she buys all kinds of fruit that she has never eaten, mangos, papayas, lychees, a pineapple and a coconut. In the cosmetics department she ignores the red nail polish.

"We have that back home, but blue and green, they would faint over that," she murmurs to herself. "I'll buy magazines, particularly the ones that specialise in music. I'll grant myself one more pleasure. I'll count the different types of toilet paper here, for fun, from white to lilac flowered, from moist to environmentally friendly. When I think of our toilet paper! ... and Mutti last year on a business trip to Poland had to take our DDR paper with her for her colleagues there."

She goes to one of the many cash desks. At all of them long queues have formed.

'Damn, couldn't they open another cash desk? I'm wasting my time here. Now that I'm in the West, I definitely don't want to have to stand in a queue.' Her gaze falls on the daily paper that she has put in her shopping trolley in passing.

' Freedom to travel soon for all DDR citizens!' reads the headline.

' They're crazy. Freedom to travel, that will never happen. Completely impossible. But if I think about the inconceivable things that have happened in the past weeks, no dream seems too Utopian any more'.

She has only just returned home, when the telephone rings. It is Ulrike, a girl from the Leipzig environmental group. She has also got away. Ulrike is calling from one of the many reception camps in which the DDR refugees are being temporarily housed.

"I'm to camp in a gymnasium from tomorrow," she says quietly into the telephone. "Do you think Sabine, we can make a go of it here? It's all so foreign to me. I want to study Psychology, at last. They didn't allow me to do that because of my parents".

Sabine gives Ulrike tips about which offices she should turn to.

"I'll send you a bit of money. I've already earned a bit extra today."

"Wow, Sabine you're a real mate. Maybe I can study in Hamburg? Then we could start up another environmental group. Bye, and thanks".

Thoughtfully, Sabine hangs up. It seems as if nobody wants to stay any longer. Lost in thought she tries her different types of yoghurt.

'Now I'll paint my nails, then I'll lie on the sofa and read the papers. Mario isn't back yet.'

It is warm and cosy in the sitting room because she has heated it thoroughly. Sabine lies on the sofa in a snug blanket. Her eyes close as she reads.

"I must still write to Thomas," she murmurs. "I'll just close my eyes for a moment." She turns the light off and falls asleep.

When she wakes up again it is pitch black.

"Strange. I don't usually sleep at this time. Are my parents eating dinner without me? It's so quiet, weird."

Sabine tries to get her bearings. "Mutti," she calls quietly. At that moment she realises that she is alone in Hamburg in Mario's flat. She stays lying motionless on the sofa. Pictures appear before her. Pictures that she has seen in the past few days on the television. Endless chains of candles, carried by thousands of people. Demonstrators holding the banners high: 'Free votes without false counting', 'Free visa to Hawaii', 'We want to live and work HERE. Free democratic elections immediately.'

A chorus of voices calls: "We are the people." Unknown people speak into microphones demanding outrageous things, for which they would have been arrested only a few weeks before.

In the meantime more and more different pictures, old people sitting silently in front of the television, nurses clothed in white hurrying down corridors. Huge supermarkets, garish boutiques with disco music. Beggars sitting in front of shopping arcades. One of them holds up a sign; 'I have no home.'

Everything seems to be spinning in front of Sabine's eyes. She pulls the blanket over her ears in order to hear no more. She covers her eyes with her hands.

"No more pictures!" Sabine calls out into the silence.

Sabine's heart thumps. She is overcome with fear. 'Has everyone forgotten me?'

There is not a sound to be heard. It is dead silent.

'Where is everyone? Have they all disappeared? But no – I'm not in Leipzig. I got out – why, actually? Because of Mutti. Where is she anyway? Oh yes she's gone to Munich with her friend. By bus. Special offer. Typical West. Special offers – we don't have them in the DDR. And Vati– have I completely forgotten him?'

Slowly the pictures reappear. She cannot fight them off. Her father appears amongst the pictures. He is standing in the bookshop with hunched shoulders. Resignedly, he is doing the stocktaking. Then she sees him sitting at home in an armchair and reading.

' He hasn't written to me once, nor to Mutti or Mario,' she thinks. 'Whenever we ring him, he hangs up. He is very bitter. I wonder if he's joined the demonstrations. Now that the whole of the DDR is out on the streets, he'll dare to do it as well. Should I call Vati?'

Sabine turns on the standard lamp.

'What, it's already 11 o'clock! Perhaps I'd better call him tomorrow. What shall I do now, I'm wide awake. Did I actually leave in order to sit around here totally alone, every evening? Life is passing me by,' she thinks, and paces up and down the flat.

In the kitchen are the opened yoghurts. 'They only made me feel sick.'

Disconsolately she puts the cartons in the fridge.

The telephone rings.

'I'd better not pick it up. Yesterday a drunkard rang and got pushy.' But the sound of the phone seems uncanny to Sabine. 'At home I was never scared but here…I'll lock the front door quickly. What else shall I do, I'll watch TV. Perhaps there'll be a good film, not a crime film though.'

However, there is neither a love film nor a crime film. The news is beginning.

'Let's see how many of us are demonstrating or who has got across the border.' Comfortably, Sabine snuggles down in the armchair.

"Good evening, Ladies and Gentlemen. The DDR has opened the border crossing points to the BRD. At 18:57 a member of the Politbüro announced the opening of the borders before journalists. Travel permits are being distributed immediately. People who want to leave the DDR can get travel visas without delay. For hours tens of thousands of East Berliners have been crossing the border virtually uncontrolled to visit the Western part of the city. They are being received with enthusiasm. Unforgettable scenes are happening at the crossing points. At the Brandenburg Gate the wall is completely losing its meaning. People are climbing unhindered up and down and walking through the gate, inaccessible since 1961. We are switching over to Berlin."

More pictures follow. Masses of people are streaming from East to West. Asked whether they want to stay in the West, they reply beaming, "No, we are only going to get a beer on the Kudamm, then home again."

Many are crying with happiness or excitement. Bewildered, they stammer, "Madness, madness."

Sabine sits motionless in front of these pictures. 'I just don't understand it. Is this supposed to be for always?'

As if the commentator had understood Sabine, he stresses that the DDR cannot afford a reversal of the free travel policy The population would not stand for it any more.

"I have really just slept through history. These ecstatic people, my people – they are no longer recognisable, they're full of life," comments Sabine on the pictures.

She sits in front of the TV, as if completely paralysed.

Strangers are dancing with each other, kissing policemen. The world is upside- down.

Long after midnight, when the test picture appears over all channels, Sabine turns off the television.

'I have just experienced the decisive moment in my life in front of the TV.' She feels sad at this thought.

'Mutti has probably tried to phone me, or Mario and I, idiot, didn't pick it up. And what if it was Thomas? Just imagine! Where might he be now, surely he has gone with others to Berlin. Perhaps he's coming to Hamburg? In any case, I'll stay up. Someone must call me.' She snuggles down under her blanket. Tears run down her face.

"Thomas, come here! Bring Julchen with you and Renate and Karin. I long to see you all. And you, Vati. Let us all be together again!"

Chapter 16

Sabine is standing at the window. She is waiting. What for? She doesn't know. Or does she?

She opens the window and peers into the street. Nobody is to be seen. Whom is she expecting? Resignedly she shuts the window. It is gradually getting dark.

Sabine has not left the flat all day. She had called in at work to say she was ill. Maria had answered the phone. "On a day like this one just isn't ill!" she had said with a laugh, "Aren't you happy?"

"Yes", she had answered quietly, "But I can't take it in yet. We were never allowed out and now that's supposed to be changing. For always. I can't believe it. If I had known that, I would never have left."

Sabine ponders about this the whole day. The departure, leaving everything behind her, was that all for nothing?

When her mother phoned from Munich this morning she had understood straight away why Sabine was so sad. She tried to comfort her. "You can really decide now where you want to live. In Hamburg or Leipzig."

"Or on the moon." she answered defiantly. Both of them had to laugh.

Mario rang her shortly afterwards. From Berlin, of course. He was really excited, and told her that he had been from West to East Berlin, and then from East to West. Everyone was received with champagne. He had climbed on to the wall, too.

"I was quite amazed at how broad the top is. I'll bring you a little piece of the wall, a brightly coloured bit."

'It could be possible that Thomas is on his way to Hamburg, today even,' thinks Sabine. This thought has been in her head for hours.

'What's the time, half past five. Perhaps I ought to go shopping, in case he comes. It doesn't matter, even if he doesn't come. I'd better hurry anyway.'

In the supermarket Sabine knows exactly what she wants today: spaghetti, tomato sauce, chocolate, fruit. By coincidence, they are all things that Thomas likes!

"One never knows," she murmurs to herself.

However, something annoys her. The people who are shopping in the supermarket behave exactly as they did yesterday. Sabine wants to call to the girl at the cash desk, "The border is open!"

But when she sees her indifferent face, she abandons the thought immediately. Sabine stands impatiently at the checkout. There she overhears two young women talking about the previous evening.

"Well, they were so happy, that was really touching. But, who knows what we can expect, if they all come over here to us. That will cost us a pretty penny. A cousin from Suhl suddenly turned up at my father's."

Heavily laden Sabine goes home, deep in thought.

'These Bundis, they've always got something to moan about. And this fear that people might take something away from them. They really have got plenty of everything.'

In a fury she stamps up the steps.

"Damn it, where are my keys?" she cries out into the silence.

"May I help you, young lady?"

Sabine jumps with fright, turns round, and looks at Thomas' laughing face. Karin and Renate are sitting on the top step. They wave to her

"Only Julchen's missing," says Sabine tonelessly, and falls weeping into Thomas' arms.

It turns into a wonderful evening. They discuss things non-stop, as they used to. The completely new political situation has given wings to their fantasies. They make boundless plans. The three of them have never been so carefree. Nothing seems impossible anymore.

At some stage they become terribly hungry. They cook mountains of spaghetti and drink champagne afterwards. Sabine had been given the bottle by one of the old people at the home "for a special occasion."

They pop the champagne cork out of the window into the dark night. They drink to their friendship; it must last forever.

Then Thomas has the crazy idea of going to the harbour. "I want to go to the docks. To the place where the ferries leave for England. Do you remember, Sabine?

In one of your first letters you sent me a photo and in the background was the ferry to England. I was really envious."

They stand for a long time on the landing stage and lose themselves in thought.

Thomas breaks the silence. "I've got a wonderful idea. From today we'll save up for a journey by ferry to England. Everything's possible now."

Thomas beams at his three friends. "Don't you want to?"

"Now he's going too far." Renate taps her forehead. "Perhaps they'll close the border again tomorrow."

"No, they can't do that, only with violence." Karin shakes her head decisively.

"You see. In one year's time we'll meet up here at this place, and then - off to England!"

"You won't get very far with your Russian," laughs Sabine. Feeling that the world belongs to them, the four friends go home.

It is long past midnight when they fall asleep, exhausted, but happy, Thomas in the armchair, Karin on the couch, Renate and Sabine in the bed in the kitchen. The next day the three of them hitchhike back to Leipzig. Sabine is a little envious. Above all, Thomas can't wait to get home.

"Let's see what's going to change. Might you come back?" he says as he leaves.

It is quite plain to Sabine that Thomas has no intention of coming to Hamburg.

Chapter 17

Leipzig, Autumn 1989

Dear Sabine,

Naturally I wanted to write to you straight after our trip to Hamburg. But events just took over, so much so that I lost all sense of time.

I think a new calendar has begun for us here: before and after the 9th November.

Luckily, I've been keeping my diary regularly. Now, on reading it through, a lot seems out of date already.

Oh, Sabine, if you could just see our teachers! They're really afraid of their pupils, some of them anyway. Just imagine, after the 9th November nearly everyone skipped school for a few days. Nobody said anything. Who knows if they went to the West, or not. There simply wasn't any school for us. And the darling of all the teachers, our super-committed FDJ-functionary, Klaus, took a week off right away. When he came back into class we were all speechless. Our colourless Klaus, always dressed in boring clothes, has turned into a genuine Bundi. Leather trousers, a garish shirt, black shoes with silver buckles. "This is the fashion now," was his comment. Suddenly Klaus has an elder sister in Cologne. She spoiled him for a week. He never spoke about his sister, he always sneered at the others, who got parcels from 'over there'.

I never cease to be amazed about who has suddenly got contacts in the West. I get the feeling that some of them dig out the most distant aunt, just to be able to boast about relatives in the West. So, our Klaus is the first turncoat I've got to know.

None of that helped him, anyway. They voted me class spokesman, not him. We held a secret election. When you think that we've never had a class spokesman before, it all happened pretty quickly.

We've changed the classroom, too. The picture of Honecker* landed in the rubbish bin, some of us even burned our schoolbooks. The seating plan has been changed. We sit in a circle opposite each other now. We've decorated our scruffy classroom walls with posters. Our wall newspaper no longer represents only one, the 'correct' opinion, but a selection of quite different ones. There isn't going to be 'one truth' for us any more. Anyway that's what our class swore.

It's a really funny situation with our teachers; nobody wants to admit anything. They are completely unsure of themselves and don't know what to teach. We're continually being asked for our opinion. That's really quite tiring. Before, they were happy when we

---

* Former DDR Head of State

kept our mouths shut, now we're supposed to examine everything critically. Despite this I still have the strange feeling that not all questions are allowed, for example, why our teachers in Staatsbürgerkunde, which incidentally has now been abolished, told us a lot of lies and dished them up as the truth.

The newly elected committee of teachers, parents and pupils has got rid of our Head. He was criticised by everyone for expelling two pupils from our school. They had been distributing pamphlets denouncing the military exercises in the school. Tomorrow a new director is being elected. We've decided on Hofmann. He was at our school for a short while and then got transferred for being too rebellious.

We've achieved even more. No pupil will stand to attention at the 'flag role call'.** The role-call was simply abolished, and with it the 'Wehrkundeunterricht***.' It's all over with fiddling with weapons and slithering around in the mud. Throwing dummy hand grenades

---

** The flag rolecall. Schools usually held them once a month (Ordnungsappell). Rolecalls were held on ceremonious occasions, on the anniversary of the DDR, of the pioneers and of the FDJ (Free German Youth), on the day celebrating freedom from Hitler's fascism on the 8th May and on the 1st May. All the pupils appeared in rank and file; the flag was hoisted in their midst.

*** Military classes. A subject from the 9th class onwards. It was supposed to prepare the boys for military service and the girls for community service. This consisted of four lessons per month and preliminary training in camps by officers of the National People's Army.

and shooting practice are forbidden, too. Now we're trying to get new schoolbooks. Just imagine, pupils are bringing books from the West with them and the teachers are really using them, and they're actually happy to do so. Well. It's all going a bit too fast for me. I still take part in the Monday Demonstrations, with Julchen. She holds up a cardboard sign that she's painted herself, with either 'For clean air' or 'No school on Saturday' on it. Yesterday morning I was quite flabbergasted. Julchen appeared for breakfast in the following garb: she'd cut a fringe along her Pioneer scarf and written loads of names of pop stars on it. Underneath that she wore her white Pioneer blouse, now painted with black skulls and crossbones. Apparently the whole class was planning to go to school like that and then to announce that they were quitting the 'Young Pioneers'. Julchen got her own way, despite resistance from Oma and went right through the town in this rig-out. Opa laughed so much at the sight of her that my mother thought he was never going to stop.

Incidentally, my mother has changed a lot. She's taken on a new lease of life. Yesterday she admitted to me that she had done my father an injustice. She wanted to force him into a career that he didn't want. She's even planning to write to him. She thought we could perhaps visit Vati. The world's upside down. Dear Sabine, best wishes for today from the first class spokesman from Leipzig. When are you coming?

Chapter 18

"Mario, can't you put something different on, it's always the scruffy jeans. Even on a day like this."

Sabine runs from the kitchen to the sitting room and back. Mario mutters to himself and disappears into the bathroom.

"Are you excited too?" Sabine asks her brother, a little later. "What if he doesn't come?"

"I don't believe he'd leave Mutti waiting at the station for nothing. Just calm down. Vati isn't a monster."

"But he never wrote."

"Now he's coming here himself. Everything's possible now. Instead of being happy you're complaining."

After half an hour Mario becomes restless, too.

"They should have been here ages ago. Come on, let's have a piece of cake." Mario helps himself.

"Perhaps they had a quarrel at the station and Vati has left straight away. After all, he's so angry with us."

When finally, after two hours, the doorbell rings frantically, Sabine and Mario can hardly believe it. The carefully laid table is looking slightly worse for wear. The cake has been cut into, bits of cake are lying on the tablecloth, the candles are burnt down, the coffee is cold.

Slowly Sabine goes to the door. "Just don't believe that it's our parents. No more disappointment." When Sabine opens the door, she stands facing her beaming parents.

"We're here." Frau Dehnert ignores her daughter's hurt face. "We're frozen through. Is there anything hot to drink?"

Without waiting for an answer she pushes her husband into the living room.

"Hello, Mario," Herr Dehnert seems embarrassed. That makes Sabine blow her top.

"We've been waiting hours for you! Could you be so kind as to explain what is going on?"

"Sabine, don't take that tone," Frau Dehnert suddenly seems nervous.

"The train was delayed. Everyone wants to travel to the West now," Herr Dehnert calms his daughter.

"First I'll make some fresh coffee," says Mario. "This has gone cold in the meantime."

"Wait Mario," Herr Dehnert says quietly. "First I would like to say how happy I am to be here with you."

Sabine swallows back, "You could have written." She senses how moved her father is.

The atmosphere still seems a bit strained when they finally sit down at the coffee table. It seems as though there is nothing to talk about. Herr Dehnert pushes his plate aside.

"I think that I owe you an explanation. I'm sure that my long silence has been a strain for you, but your leaving was not less of one for me. At the time I couldn't understand it all. Perhaps I could understand Mario's case most of all, with Mutti it was discussed but I couldn't understand Sabine's. I didn't want to admit that for you there was a life worth living on the other side of the border. When you went one after another, I was scared of the gossip of neighbours, colleagues and friends. I believed that they'd despise me because I couldn't keep my family together."

Herr Dehnert clears his throat. His voice sounds husky. Slowly he pours a cup of coffee and takes a sip, puts the cup down and is silent.

Frau Dehnert becomes tense. "Go on, please."

"Yes, well, I was really wrong about the people around me. No one criticised me, the opposite. There has been almost no one in recent months who has not asked himself whether he should leave our country. One colleague asked me whether I thought parents should have the right to stop their children from escaping. We all knew clearly that over there they have less chance to shape their lives independent of State pressures. Didn't we force our children to accept things which they justifiably did not want to go along with? Didn't we persuade them to fit in, not to draw attention to themselves, to join the army and to study an unpopular subject? Didn't we keep quiet when they asked us why we always went on holiday to the Baltic but never drove to the North Sea?"

"If we had ever managed to get a holiday place at the Baltic," interrupts Frau Dehnert.

"Mutti, Vati means it in a symbolic way," interrupts Sabine.

"Don't interrupt me all the time," says Herr Dehnert. "My colleague said he could understand why his children left. He only reproached himself that it had to come so far.

Don't we have to thank our children for the freedom which has come about through the opening of the border?" Herr Dehnert looks at Mario and Sabine.

"I've thought for a long time about this conversation with my colleague. If hundreds of thousands of young people hadn't left our country, so that it seemed that the stream of refugees would never dry up, I'm sure that the borders would not have been opened. This mass exodus has bled our country dry. In order to put a stop to it, the DDR citizens were granted the freedom to travel. In order to prevent a catastrophe, something decisive had to be done. It was not possible to bring in tanks in order to prevent the fleeing people. The people had decided not to go on living like that and so no power would have held them back."

"You mean that our escape wasn't for nothing? So everything wasn't in vain?" Mario leans back with a sigh. "I've often asked myself whether everyone despises me because I left. I was afraid they think that I simply dropped out."

"Exactly," Sabine agrees with her brother. "And even today I still don't know where I belong. My hometown is Leipzig. Until a short time ago, Hamburg was foreign to me. Now I live in Hamburg and feel divided in two. One day I think that it doesn't matter where I live, the main thing is that I feel good. The next day I would prefer most of all to get on the first train to Leipzig and stay there. On the other hand, on the third day I think that I'll never return again because I couldn't bear the feeling of being shut in any longer. However now, with the border open, I no longer know what I want. My first thought was, you'll go back straight away. However then came the letter of admittance for Psychology, whereupon I was incredibly happy. Now I don't know at all what I want."

"Let's ask Mutti where she wants to live now?" Herr Dehnert looks at his wife questioningly.

"With my family," she replies diplomatically.

Sabine thinks that her mother makes it all too simple for herself. Clearly she is avoiding the decision.

'If she went back, perhaps I would go, too. But no, it's difficult to return to my parents,' thinks Sabine.

"I thought," Frau Dehnert puts her coffee cup energetically on the table. "I'd go travelling around the Mediterranean in the summer and then…"

"Then you could actually come back to Leipzig," Herr Dehnert interrupts his wife. "Now you can travel from home."

"Yes, but the children still need me, don't they?"

Mario and Sabine are silent. Her mother must have noticed that they have in the meantime coped quite well alone.

"Christa, the children have become completely independent. Now let them go their own ways. I believe that we both have to learn that our children have grown up."

"I don't know." Frau Dehnert looks indecisively at her children who are sitting on the sofa smiling, embarrassed.

"Would you find it so dreadful living with me? It went quite well before." Herr Dehnert puts his arms around his wife tenderly. "The flat is quite empty without you. Could you ever imagine living in Leipzig again one day?" Herr Dehnert looks at his children enquiringly.

"I'll have to see," murmurs Mario. "One has got used to certain standards. It's still too backward over there for me."

"Now wait a minute, what do you mean by that?" Herr Dehnert looks at his son, irritated.

"What can I do over there? It is simply too boring for me in Leipzig. The people here are more relaxed."

"More relaxed, if that's all," Herr Dehnert interrupts his son.

"Well, more free. The people here have seen the world, are informed and are not so bourgeois as over there. I'm really ashamed when I see our people walking around laden with plastic bags. They buy everything, find everything great and don't have a clue about anything."

"How can you speak like that about us?" Frau Dehnert says indignantly. "You've only been in the West a few weeks more than us, don't forget that. Others are as capable as you of learning."

"Now don't get into a huff," Sabine calms her mother down. "I can understand Mario. Over there it's boring for young people. School, studies, work, nothing else."

Herr Dehnert is annoyed. "I think you're being unfair. I didn't have the feeling that you were constantly bored at home."

"No. But I can't imagine living in Leipzig any longer. It's all so familiar."

"Two minutes ago, you said you didn't know where you should live. On top of that, since the 9th November a few things have already changed at home. You both really should come back soon. No one needs you here. But at home you're needed. Now we have the chance to build something new. But if there aren't enough people…"

The phone rings. Sabine picks it up. It is Maria.

"Hello, will you come with me to the cinema? My brother's coming too, and afterwards he's taking us to a new discotheque."

Maria is disappointed at Sabine's refusal, but despite this she says, "It's great that you're together again. You wanted it so much. Tell me, I've been wanting to ask you for a long time, will you show me Leipzig?"

"I don't really know whether you'd like it there."

"How come? Then I won't show you Volos, my hometown, in the summer. Who knows whether you'll like it there?"

"That's blackmail!" Sabine has to laugh. How uncomplicated Maria is, laid-back, as Mario would say. Maria always says, "You Germans are usually so serious, never funny or spontaneous."

"Oh gosh, if Maria comes to Leipzig! Everyone goes around with even grumpier faces than here. Will she enjoy herself there?"

Chapter 19

"In an hour we'll be in Leipzig."

"At last," answers Maria. She stretches out on the seat and yawns. "It's high time".

"Before, you'd have needed longer. People were searched for hours on the border."

"I know, because of smuggling. Like in Greece".

"You know what annoys me like mad about you Wessis? You have no idea about the DDR, but you always come out with a smart answer. You always think you know better. I wasn't allowed to come near this border, for example. If I'd tried to cross the border illegally, I'd have landed in Bautzen[*]. How often have I longingly watched the trains as they went into the West? Just get in, I said to myself. So, OK, they'll throw you out at the border. Did you know that we didn't even have our own passports?"

---

[*] A prison in the former DDR

She speaks louder because she has the feeling that Maria is not listening to her at all.

"Sabine, you know what upsets me?" Maria's voice sounds rather hurt. "That you always say 'we' and mean the DDR. You don't live in this country any more. Perhaps the DDR won't exist for much longer. It looks as if the borders will finally come down, so you mustn't keep the border up by artificial means."

Silently Sabine looks out of the window. The first suburbs of Leipzig appear.

'How shabby everything looks here. I'd forgotten. So grey, but also very familiar,' thinks Sabine, a little depressed. 'What a long time I've needed to return, and even then only on a visit. I wanted to go right away in November, and now it's already spring. Thomas, Renate and Karin have often been to Hamburg, but I couldn't decide whether to come. If I'm honest, I had less and less inclination to go back. But why? Everything that's being found out now. The spying that was going on everywhere, people after personal gain.

Nobody admits to have been involved, everyone was a victim. Why doesn't anyone stand by what he has done? I wouldn't like to know what our Frau Müller tells people - probably that she was forced to do everything.

How often have I thought recently about Tante Gretchen, my godmother in Dresden. When I was small she was always telling me about her great love in Cologne. How she would have liked to have visited him. But she wasn't allowed to. In the photos he had a great uniform on, like a prince. When I was bigger, I realised that he was a carnival prince. Now it's too late for a visit. Tante Gretchen died suddenly last year, without having seen her prince again. How glad she would have been about the opening of the border.'

Deep in thought, Sabine looks out of the window.

"Looks a bit miserable here," complains Maria.

"Station areas always look like this. Just don't complain about everything. We have to get out in a minute."

Maria looks out of the window. Suddenly she waves.

"Hi, Thomas. He's there," she announces, beaming.

"I could hardly have missed hearing that." Sabine answers sharply.

Then she is hugged animatedly by Maria. "Come on, don't be angry. Let's have a few lovely days in your Leipzig."

Thomas, grinning broadly, hands a bouquet to Maria and Sabine.

"We never had flowers here before." Sabine is still in a bad mood.

"Who's moaning here?" Maria says challengingly.

'If only I hadn't brought her with me. She just doesn't understand anything,' thinks Sabine crossly. She comes to a standstill, shocked. "Thomas, election posters for the SPD. But that's forbidden!"

"Look," Thomas pulls some magazines out of his bag. "I've even bought 'Bravo' for Julchen, 'the Spiegel' for Opa and the TV magazine with the West programmes for Mutti."

Sabine smiles, embarrassed.

"I've brought you a load of forbidden things, too. All the books that were on your list and were forbidden here before, and the newest comics. Goodness Thomas, pinch me. It's so great that I'm here."

"At last you're looking a bit more cheerful," Maria links arms with both of them. "In the train you were unbearable. Now I'm hungry. Over there you can get hamburgers. Hurry up; I'm dying of hunger."

Thomas and Sabine look at each other and laugh. Hamburgers in Leipzig, that's twice as funny.

"Standing in a queue, nothing's changed there," sighs Sabine, as they finally reach their turn. "Where shall we go? My father's not home yet."

"We can go to the Eiscafe Pinguin and drink a 'Blue Hour'!"

Sabine chokes with laughter on her hamburger. Maria looks on uncomprehendingly. Thomas staggers up and down in front of the two girls and groans, "I'm so dizzy, I feel so sick."

Thomas sways about so deceptively genuinely that an older woman looks after him, shaking her head.

'Now they've all gone crazy here,' thinks Maria.

They walk through the town. Sabine notices the advertising straightaway. Coca-Cola seems to be everywhere. Video shops, political posters and adverts for films that she never would have thought would be shown in Leipzig.

'Bundi go home' was written on the front of a West German bank. Sabine finds the big, painted letters threatening. 'Do they mean me too?'

Thomas interrupts her thoughts. "Do you know what's really crazy? Do you see the Stasi canteen back there? It's been built into a huge disco with all the trimmings."

"Stasi*, what kind of company is that?" asks Maria bored. Sabine and Thomas look at each other, taken aback, and explode with laughter. Maria looks at them both blankly.

In the next few days Sabine hardly has time to think, because Thomas has planned almost every hour. He wants to show her all the changes. On the last day she goes on strike. The last day should belong to her alone. Sabine needs time to think. She is at home in her bedroom. Everything looks exactly the same as when she left it nine months before. Sabine considers what she should take with her back to Hamburg, she left so many things behind. To Hamburg. She brooded for a long time. Should she stay in Leipzig or go back?

'Shouldn't I stay here? Help my country, especially now? There are more meaningful occupations than studying Psychology in Hamburg.' Sabine thinks about it a lot.

However, Leipzig has already become a little bit foreign to her. She doesn't feel as effortlessly at home there as she had thought she would. Many friends are in the West too, and they don't want to return. They don't feel any obligation towards their country.

'To help with the reconstruction,' thinks Sabine. 'Haven't I heard that before, ad nauseam? Why shouldn't I think of myself now? Especially as they could have let me study what I wanted, back then. If so much has changed already, I want to be able to make the decisions

---

* "Stasi": Colloquial term for State Security Service

as to where I live and what I study.' Sabine rummages around in her chest of memories, deep in thought.

'I can definitely throw out the FDJ badge, but I'll keep my sports awards. If I stayed here, everything would be more difficult. Karin, for example, doesn't know what she ought to study. She was admitted for law, but now that subject is the first to have been abolished. No one knows exactly how things should continue.'

Sabine had criticised her friends for having so little imagination. She has the feeling that they are still waiting for someone to tell them what they should do. "Arrogant West-girl!" Renate roared at her.

She couldn't calm down again.

"Do you know what we call you?" Renate asked Sabine furiously. "Besserwessis."

Sabine looked at her friend speechlessly.

"Oh, sorry. I don't mean you, but the others from over there. I've had enough. Before the 9th November I wasn't allowed to study what I wanted. After the 9th November I can't study because I have to earn money. My father's unemployed and my mother's afraid she'll be made redundant. So I have to work as well. We can forget about our trip to Spain. My father got really infuriated yesterday, because one of you said on the television that people from the DDR are really not used to working. My father roared "With your ultra modern West machines we could have done hard work too."

Sabine closes the chest again. 'The things can stay here. I'll come and see Vati often, then I can still think about what to take with me. Luckily my relationship with Vati has improved a lot. Since I knew about the story with his refusal to enter the party, I really admire him. Perhaps I should actually say that to him.'

When Thomas drops in in the evening both of them get back to the subject of the DDR straight away. "You know, Sabine, up until now our lives were predetermined. We didn't have to take care of anything ourselves. Neither a university place nor a room in a student house. Studies were just an extended time at school, everything was dictated. After that you had a guaranteed job. Decisions were made for us. And now? I have the feeling that I'm walking straight down a long street and suddenly side streets are appearing everywhere. I can actually use these ones; however I don't know where they lead to. Perhaps it's a dead end. I feel unsure. I have to ask about everything. How do you do that, how much does it cost?

Before, we felt quite happy in the collective, it wasn't only obligation. Now I have to learn to say "I want" and not "we want" any longer. Do you know how the Wessis recognise us? By the make of our jeans, by the beige-grey shoes and the short, quilted jackets. We all carry crumpled plastic bags. We all stand patiently, equipped like this in a queue in front of Aldi. That's what the newspapers are writing about us over there. And there's more.

Instead of working, we go shopping. Affluency can't come fast enough. You know, Sabine, I'd rather stay here, if you have such an opinion of us. It's never said that we've not only gained but that we've also lost something. For example the community, we had no worries about unemployment or having a serious lack of housing." Thomas works himself up into such a rage, that he doesn't notice how furious Sabine is.

"Yes, sure, the beloved collective, so very snug and loveable. Wasn't it rather that the collective determined what opinion one should have, what one was allowed to believe, what one had to read? One didn't need to think any more. And then always the pictures of the poor people in Capitalism, no one cares for the other there. Exploitation, unemployment, crime, that was how the West was portrayed to us. A cold, heartless world.

You're not thinking straight. Stay in your oh so ideal world! I'm happy that I don't have to live with you lot any more!" Sabine roars, then she weeps and her face turns red.

Thomas is embarrassed, he hadn't wanted that.

"Please stop your bawling. If we talk at cross-purposes, how on earth are others going to manage? You're one of us! Listen to me. I was so happy when the border opened. On my first journey to Hamburg, I thought I was growing wings. I hoped that now I could do everything that I'd always wanted. That state of euphoria has left me now. I'm afraid of being laughed at by people in the West, of not being accepted by them. Every day we hear that our Abi is worthless, our knowledge is one-sided, we can't speak English, computers are Greek to us, our cars are cardboard, the tram prices too low. I can't bear to hear it any longer. Everyone fears for his work place, it's quite dreadful.

I hadn't thought that a new beginning would be so difficult. For example a few of us have founded a school club. We wanted to discuss the changes to our school.

At first it was quite exciting, but at some stage we didn't know what to talk about. Then the club broke up.

I can see what you're thinking. You know yourself that we learnt nothing about advocating our own opinions. Someone must help us. Many people have already completely adapted. They accept everything without criticism."

Both of them are sitting in Sabine's former bedroom and seem strangely lost. Hiding in the bookshelf is a small brown bear from childhood days. The poster of a long forgotten music group is hanging on the otherwise bare wall. The problems of the whole world seem to rest on Sabine and Thomas.

"You know, Julchen has visited our father with my grandparents. The first thing that Julchen said to him when she saw his flat was, "You're not actually living in a castle!" For her, her dad was rich and the rich live in castles. She believed this because he always sent her lovely things and looked so elegant in the photos. Oma had secretly shown us the pictures; Mutti wasn't allowed to know. Can you believe it, my parents are phoning each other? Mutti said, with a blush, that it was only because of the children. It would be wonderful if they could get back together again. Don't you think so?"

"You see, there's something good for you after all in this new time." Sabine cannot stop herself from making the sharp remark.

"Above all, that you're here. When I can't talk about everything, I feel like I'm suffocating. Do you understand? It's actually a great time that we're experiencing. We were never allowed to get away. I remember exactly how I was standing, last year, in Warnemünde, on the beach and looking longingly after the ferry to Denmark. That was forbidden for us. Now I don't know where I should travel to first. So many things are open to me, but which way should I choose to go? Help me Sabine! I'm so afraid of going under."

Comfortingly, Sabine puts her arm around her friend.

'The self-confident Thomas,' thinks Sabine. 'He's really tormenting himself.'

"You know Thomas, you don't have to make choices today for the rest of your life. If you don't know what you ought to do, then think about what you would enjoy."

"But Sabine, what I would enjoy – that's no life perspective."

"My goodness, don't take it so seriously. We're not even twenty and you're already thinking about your pension! You must develop a bit of fantasy. I think you have real comical talent; perhaps you should join the circus? It's as if your grandfather is younger than you!"

"That's right," sighs Thomas, "He's learning Italian now. He wants to go to Venice with Oma in the summer, to make up for their honeymoon. At seventy!"

Chapter 20

"Hey look, a Trabi."

"Where? You must have sunstroke. No, how amazing, a real Trabi, in Greece! Nikos, hoot the horn."

Sabine nudges Maria's brother. He puts on a veritable hooting concert.

"After three weeks the first Trabi. You see, the dream to travel to Greece wasn't only yours." Maria smiles at Sabine.

"Oh," sighs Sabine, "It was such a wonderful holiday. It's such a shame we have to go home already."

"Well, I'm looking forward to Hamburg. This constant heat in Greece is unbearable. I can't stand the food any longer either."

"Our Granny," Nikos taps his forehead and shakes his head. "Sabine is the Greek on this holiday, not you. You got worked up about things the whole time. Unbelievable! The beach wasn't clean, the food was too oily, the disco boring, the people pushy. It was lucky Sabine was here. With you my dear sister, this holiday was an absolute strain."

Sabine laughs, Maria looks out of the window, insulted.

"I know that feeling. In Leipzig I could only complain too; Maria, on the other hand, found everything funny and unusual. She polished off Bockwurst in huge quantities, and even drank beer."

Nikos nods, pacified. The countryside glides past them, they are nearing the Yugoslavian border. Sabine daydreams.

'Here in Greece I felt as though I was really living for the first time. Perhaps I'm exaggerating, but I have never felt so good before.' Sabine thinks back longingly over the last few weeks. She swam in the sea for the first time. Maria practically had to use force to drag her out.

"You must have webbed feet," she said nastily, but she was proud that her friend was enjoying herself so much.

She was welcomed by Maria's family like a long lost daughter. She didn't feel for a moment like a stranger. She had to tell her story to everyone, particularly about where the dream of Greece came from. The booklet *'Greece and its Islands'* was passed around until it was almost falling apart. It had been with her the whole time, during the escape and now in Greece. Sabine spoke a lot about Thomas, about her family. Maria patiently translated. She had to tell Maria's grandmother twice about the flight over the Hungarian border, she was so impressed by it. During the story she crossed herself many times. The next day she handed Sabine a book with a brightly coloured binding. A diary. The grandmother wanted her to write down everything that she had experienced in the past months. That way she would always remember it.

Sabine pulls the diary out of her bag. Yesterday evening she wrote in it for the first time:

Departure from Greece.

Tomorrow we travel to Hamburg. Do I really want to go back?

Where is my home? Perhaps in Leipzig after all? Or would I prefer to live here in this small Greek village? Question after question.

For Maria's grandmother it is simple. Wherever her family is that's also her home, she says. For Maria, on the other hand, friends and work are more important than her Greek family in the village. Nikos wants to return to the village, but not until he is old, like his parents will do.

And me? Where do I belong? Soon there will be no more border between both of our German countries. We will be one country then. I don't actually have to decide any more which part I want to live in, whether in the East or in the West. From a distance, here in Greece, it all seems much simpler. I could study in Hamburg, later teach at the school in Leipzig and spend my holidays alternately in Hungary and Greece. No one can stop me and I don't need to apply for a travel permit any more.

I can send Renate a tape of BAP and she can play the music to anyone, without having to be worried that someone will tell on her. Karin can tell me on the telephone how her brother got on in prison, and no one can listen in. It doesn't matter if they do.

Her brother was released from prison prematurely, because the offence 'escape from the Republic' no longer exists.

I don't have to worry about voicing my opinions any more, even when others are against them. I'll have to get used to that.

I am going to try, and that will really be my goal, to unite both parts in myself, East and West. Perhaps something new will arise out of that. It could be that in ten years time I am just as much at home in New York as in Moscow. Borders can no longer confine me.

Sabine claps her diary shut
'Will I be able to do all that?'
She is becoming quite dizzy at the thought.
She is overcome by a pleasant tiredness. As if through a wall of mist she hears Maria call:
"Look Sabine, another Trabi."

Chronological Table of Events.

1989

7th May: Elections to the Volkskammer ('People's Chamber') in the DDR. Citizens' rights and peace groups observe the counting and ascertain massive corruption.

Summer: Start of the mass flight from the DDR. Refugees in the embassies of the Federal Republic in Prague, Warsaw and Budapest.

10th September: The Hungarian Government announces that from the 11th September on, all DDR citizens wanting to leave may travel directly from Hungary to the country of their choice.

11th September: The start of a colossal movement of refugees from Hungary to Bavaria.

End of September - beginning of October: After travel restrictions between the DDR and Hungary: rush to the embassies in Prague and Warsaw. On account of the imminent 40th anniversary celebrations, the DDR allows thousands of special trains from Prague and

Warsaw to travel to the Federal Republic. Tumultuous scenes on DDR stations as the trains go through. Numerous arrests, brutal police action in Dresden.

2nd October: 2500 people demonstrate in Leipzig. They are driven apart by reservists.

7th October: Celebration of the 40th anniversary of the DDR. Demonstrations in many towns for reforms. Dispersal by police .

9th October: About 7000 people demonstrate in the Nikolaikirche after the traditional 'Peace Prayers' for democratic reforms. "We are the people."

18th October: Erich Honecker is removed as SED-General Secretary and Chairman of the State Council. His successor is Egon Krenz.

23rd October: Huge demonstrations for reforms in many towns of the DDR.

4th November: Hundreds of thousands demonstrate on the streets of Berlin. Authors, artists and representatives of the new organisations give speeches.

9th November: SED-Politbüro member Günther Schabowski, announces unexpectedly in the evening, the opening of the border crossings to the West from the next day onwards. Thousands storm to the Wall during the night and enforce free border crossing.

1990

18th March: Elections for the People's Chamber in the DDR. Overwhelming majority for the coalition of the CDU, Liberals and Demokratischer Aufbruch.

18th May: Signing of the State Treaty between the DDR and the BRD.

6th June: Local elections in the DDR.

1st July: The currency and social union of both German states comes into effect.

3rd October: According to article 23 of the Basic Law, the DDR-Länder, Sachsen, Thüringen, Sachsen-Anhalt, Brandenburg and Mecklenburg-Vorpommern join the BRD.

2nd December: Election for a mutual German Parliament.

About the Translators

Louisa Barnett, Kitty Geddes and Lizzie Scott, former pupils of Tudor Hall School in Banbury, studied the novel 'Ich fühl mich so fifty-fifty' for their A2 exam in German literature, which they sat in June 2004. Aware that there was no translation into English of the book, they decided to do it themselves in their final school year. They found the project hard work, but very rewarding. All three have travelled many times to Germany and Austria, and they love the German language. Karin König, the book's author, delighted by the girls' enthusiasm, has fully supported their project.

Diana Hughes (German teacher)

Cover photograph of Camilla Russell,
by Alicia de Haldevang; also former students of
German at Tudor Hall, June 2005.